MARTIN
FARRELL

MARTIN FARRELL

A TALE OF THE REIVERS

JANNI HOWKER

RED FOX

A Red Fox Book

Published by Random House Children's Books
20 Vauxhall Bridge Road, London SW1V 2SA

A division of Random House UK Ltd
London Melbourne Sydney Auckland
Johannesburg and agencies throughout the world

Cover illustration by Dave McKean from *Reivers!*,
an audio-visual show at Tullie House Museum, Carlisle
© Carlisle City Council

Designed by Douglas Martin

1 3 5 7 9 10 8 6 4 2

First published in Great Britain by Julia MacRae 1994

Red Fox edition 1997

Printed and bound in Great Britain by
Cox & Wyman Ltd, Reading, Berkshire

RANDOM HOUSE UK Limited Reg. No. 954009

Papers used by Random House UK Limited
are natural, recyclable products made from wood grown in
sustainable forests. The manufacturing processes conform to
the environmental regulations of the country of origin.

ISBN 0 09 918161 4

The author would like to thank
Northern Arts and the Authors' Foundation
for their generous support.

AUTHOR'S NOTE

Although the Debatable Land is an historical and
geographical area of the Western March of the Border and many
of the names in this story are still current in this area, this
is not an historical novel. The events, characters, and typography
are as fictional as the dialect of the storyteller.

FOR MICK

The Borders of darkness will never be closed
To the smugglers of light . . .

This ae night, this ae night,
  Every nighte and alle,
  Fire, and sleet, and candle-lighte,
And Christe receive thye saule.

A Lyke-wake dirge

This man, he had no sort of name to waste breath on, he filled his mouth with drink. A swig and a slug before he had come through the door and like a horse at a trough at the wedding feast. Oh, he would still be alive right enough but for the night he got drunk and his voice carried.

'Nails O' God! You dun mean thas, man!' he says. 'You dun mean to say he's thinking he's the first wi' her!'

Who heard it? Will Armstrong didn't. He was gone from the hall by then. So was she, his new wife. Anne, they called her. An Eliot by a Nixon who was half-cousin to the Old Man.

And if the Old Man had've been there? If he'd heard *that*! Would there have been blood in the hall half dousing the fire? A great swilling of flagstones, a huge sluicing of steps to be carried on before those newly-weds could have risen and come down all soft treading on their linen-clean soles?

But no. It wasn't the Old Man heard the drunk. What does that matter? Someone did. He was dead the day after. No one thought much about it. Pathetic. A Farrell. A Farrell bare-shanked out of Ireland, so they said, taken up with a widow.

It was Jock's Alan, an Eliot, who heard him. Couldn't stomach the insult to the young bride, his fair cousin.

Next day, the drunk, the one they called Farrell, he had no tongue. The rest of him was in the sty. Not murder, exact. He was alive when they slung him in there. The black boar did the rest.

So then, it was some wedding. Mostly it went well, if we forget about Farrell. A rare feast! The guests most lived to go home and were happy. They knew that if nothing else were to make much of their lives they'd still seen this event. It was one for the grandchildren. An Eliot wed to an Armstrong and connected through Nixons to Old Man Armstrong himself!

The most of the guests were in the Old Man's black mail. They paid black money, protection, to keep his fire from their rooves and their doors. Did they squint at the wedding with one weather-eye for what it might mean – these guests who had been to two weddings before? Now, not one of those bridegrooms, sons of this house, wasn't talking to worms.

The eldest was hanged by the Grahams, the second dead of a fever got from his dog. And never a grandchild got from the two. So here was the youngest away to his bed with a bonny young bride.

In whispers, the guests even talked about *harvest!* It was only a *shussh* of a sound like the screep of Nottingham lace against the hard heelskin of our bride's wee foot. Just a wee nothing of a noise like that. Yet enough to rouse a man's body, to set a belly yearning. *Harvest.*

For too many years it had meant black smoke and black crows like great cinders pecking toasty grains in black fields. And threshing? A grim joke. Some man tossed up on pikes till the wind blew away the chaff of his cries.

And why? You ask, why? Because at the wedding of that second son, a joke about horses offended Eliots and Nixons, leaving Armstrongs alone in their feud with the Grahams.

Harvest.

It went along the hall like a breeze ripple on barley and everyone there knew it was only Anne Eliot's yellow heels and Nottingham lace made that word touch their lips at all.

Or maybe it was Will Armstrong's beard that night. He'd taken a horse brush to it and had himself a good grooming. Long, long strokes down to make it lie against his throat and chest. And it lay down, combed gold, his lips like

2

a red sun above. Ah, the guests could have sighed and stooked it, all those hard men watching. It made them want to go out into the stableyard and snare out the cotters in their own tangly stuff.

And the gangling boys there, no beards at all – should have been in their beds the whole silly tribe of them – they just stroked and stroked at their own poxy chins, thinking softness and white bread and breasts. But then, let's pipe a fair tune for them, not one of them remembered a true harvest – the prickle and sweat of it.

If the Old Man had've been there, those lads would have stopped twitching, sat still as hares. *His* beard was cinders, smoke, grey ash, like a burning of fields seen across a river – the sky drizzle, the mist choking. And his eyes, Old Man Armstrong's, they were stone eyes. No colour. Maybe a bit yellow, a bit milk blue. They only ever opened one at a time, like the moon between clouds. He did all his watching across the Border like that.

But no. He wasn't there at his own son's wedding. He'd not been to a one of his three lads' nuptials. He had no stomach for it. Too often, before the fiddler had sobered, he'd to be out riding, making widows and orphans of some of his guests. Once, of a daughter-in-law still tasting her first kiss.

What was said this night by that wee man Farrell was something he missed and no bit body troubled to tell him, thinking the drunk dealt with and the least of the guests.

So then. It was a fine grand ceremonious roast-swan-and-venison on the table affair, this wedding of Anne Eliot and Will Armstrong. And all the guests' weapons stacked like a briar hedge in the rack by the door. Which isn't to say each man didn't have a slim knife concealed some place up his sleeve or in a boot top, even in nosegays, among the fair ladies.

Who wasn't invited? Aye, at a wedding, ye'd be wise to take note! Which of your neighbours has fallen foul of this feasting and this winter might starve? Which head of a household deigns not to come – still sworn to black feud with the Armstrongs' great hall? The Warden sent word that an affliction of his long English throat must keep him away. Truth? Ha! He wrote the same night to the Queen saying how he'd been rendered speechless that such villains and horse-thieves could dare him to come!

Sharp as a spindle that might prick a finger was the place not set for one neighbour – the Widow, Margaret Graham. Whisht . . . They said in the wood, where those four ill-starred Grahams were slain by the Armstrongs, every tree's dead. And what the Armstrongs stole from her daughter, no man can return. Fifteen summers ago the only bushels of barley saved from feud burnings were those drenched in blood.

Why should these guests fear her? She's no menfolk to avenge her. Yet, there's a chill place on the flagstones. Aye, her presence still stood.

But away! Away! This is a wedding! On a fine August evening. A good time, gentle, moonlight enough to stop men hiding fists and intentions, and the cattle to be heard after midnight out on the hills crunching the sweet grass.

Everything peaceful in the Debatable Lands. The Galloway fiddler (he'd been brought here at dagger point) at last gave in to his kidnap. He wiped the fear sweat off his chin, set his music into a tuck of his neck and dropped his shoulder. That way he played in the dawn as sweet as a thrush.

Anne Eliot, in the tower, she heard him as she lay with her hand in her husband's fine beard. She didn't dare move a finger for fear of tugging the whiskers caught in her rings, but then, she wasn't inclined to.

She heard that little bit of commotion, some hooves clattering – maybe three horses – a man grunting protest in a steam of drink. She set nothing by it. It wasn't a saddling of mounts – a big riding. It was only Farrell, a name meaning nothing to no one being taken to his last home. Nothing to be thought of. So, no, she was full of soft notions, her womb like rose-water. She traced, without touching, the golden field of her husband's belly until the dawn wind, blowing down from the North, made her stretch a white hand for the coverlet to take the chill off her back.

Is it true what they say? That the Widow saw it all in a drop of well water she splashed on her mirror, keeked at each guest in his chair in the droplets' clear shiver, watched Will Armstrong and Anne Eliot's love-play?

There's smoke in the rumours of small men, for the grief of a great woman to whom such wrongs had been done must be feared in the night like a cursing, and a man makes a wee cross with his fingers to avert such an eye. Let's just say that among the throng of the wedding, Margaret Graham had her own way to spy.

This man, the drunk – aye, I'll waste a bit breath on him. This man, Farrell, he had a stepson. What a thing to think on! He'd no more kin than that. Was it a shame or a mercy? I'll leave ye to judge.

The child had brought him a living and been a path to his death. It was the only thing he had saving the horse Jock's Alan roped him to to bring him on home. And home? A turf house on an outrim of moor, curlew and bog and the peat-cutter's black trench, two pigs, two cows, a duster of hens, no track and no fence.

Was it his land? Ask Old Man Armstrong.

This boy was called Martin – this stepson. Martin Farrell. No one passed by so who knew his name? His mother? Come closer. Let me tell in a whisper. *She was a Graham but she's thirteen years dead.*

She never lived long enough to give the wee babe a sister, let alone an army of brothers to stand alongside him in the fray. How could she?

She died, her boy crawling to stand at her knee, in that harvest when Armstrongs and Grahams set enough fire between England and Scotland to turn horizons Biblical and prayers were said as far down as Penrith.

What did she die of?

Looking at her man.

She was threading a needle to mend a bridle when she saw Farrell through the eye of it, sat slummocked, snoring, half asleep. And this on a night when every hill of the West March blazed a beacon that had been torched from the cinder in her heart.

For all the lick and twist she put on her twine she could not get that needle threaded, and knowing, aye, owning, she'd lost her squint on the future, she took sudden and died.

So that left the boy. Thirteen years on he had skinny brown ribs and motherless cotters in his dark chestnut hair. Once in a while, he would count on his fingers, one, two, three up to nine, dithering the tenth one as he ran out of counters, wondering how many months it takes to get born.

It was a reckoning of fathers he was after. Who could be his one? He lived like a thorn tree with the wind in his ears — the one mortal voice being Farrell's to tell him how he got to be grown in that place.

I was wed to your mother but yer no my get.

One, two, three, up to nine till ten lifted both hands up in front of his face. Ach, leave the lad be! When he lowers his fingers what does he see? There in the straw, the black cow licking the knob fur between the ears of her calf.

So then. His mother, what had he of her? A ring, such a wee thing, thin as a beech leaf in autumn, twiddled with letters. He knew nothing of them. It was kept in a pouch tucked in his shirt.

And of Farrell, his step-father, what did he know? That he wore a rag at his throat to hide the scar on his neck. How had he got it?

I fell from a tree tangled in rope, swopped an honest hemp noose for the damn halter of thee.

Each Michaelmas a stranger came with gold to pay for six sleds of stacked peat. A transaction of whispers. Martin once heard his name and kenned in that instant that it was never just the dry sod being sold. So, he watched the men's brown lips pucker like purses and wondered where among curlew and bog-rush they thought might be ears.

Aye, Martin Farrell, at fourteen years old, he might be some raven hatched on a cliff face and raised by the stones.

On the dawn of that wedding, he'd watched the man,

Farrell, ride for the hall, though never invited. A man bloated and bleary and swilled up with lost pride.

Wi' what I ken, can they turn me away!

It was the last he saw of him, and our lad? He had a fine time hunting the rabbits on that peaceable day.

But now the moon's risen. It's the night of the wedding. What will befall him? Listen. I'll tell.

It's midnight. He thinks the wind woke him when he hears the hoof gallop that broke him from dreams. Away! He stands in alarm to face the black stranger on horseback who's kicked open the door. Martin Farrell backs up to the fire-embers away from the hooves of the trampling grey mare.

'Get up! Get up!' the stranger cried and caught him by the arm. 'Hup! Hup!' He hauled the lad between his knees and galloped over the moss. Martin's breath was banged from his body, his thoughts knocked from his head. He was slung across the saddle-horn with a fist knotted in his shirt.

That's how it happened. Two lots of guests rode from that feast – one to bring the step-father and one to take the son, and only a moon scud of shadow between them. If Jock's Alan had felt Martin's bed when he got there, he'd have found it still warm.

And if Martin Farrell had heard anything over the thunder of his heart and the hooves, what would he have heard? The wee man Farrell shriek a warning, sob a damnation cut off by a scream. But how could he hear that? He was to hear nothing but the blood in his ears until dawn stood red on the moor's rim, and the mare was reined at last to a stand.

'She was a Graham,' said the black stranger, as Martin twisted in his grasp. 'The Crow's robbed a strange nest.'

Martin saw the twin snotteries of the big man's nose, each hair of his whiskers black against the pink sky.

'My mother?' Martin whispered, hard put to speak, even his voice was as blue as a bruise. 'Are we kin?' He'd a sudden inkling he'd got none.

What was his answer? A great gusting laugh as he's dropped from the saddle! A glimpse of the hair-fringed hooves cutting moons in the peat as the mare rears away. Then the stranger was gone.

Some say that when the lad stood to stare after, he saw nothing but a black bird flying northward on the morning's red wind, and neither horse nor rider was there to be seen.

But away! Away! Enough of such tales. What was there to be done? The lad didn't want to find out. But he'd learned from the hare and the leveret the art to stay still until fear shadows sweep by. So he came to his courage, washed his bruising with dew, then set his back to the sun and turned towards home. That was no short walk and near as far as ever he'd travelled since he was born.

It was noon when he got there, and what did he find? A mound of fresh earth under the thorn tree there by the door, and the Galloway fiddler sitting beside it, playing a slow tune.

He stopped when he saw Martin, then lifted his bow and started again. But could he play on? The look in the boy's eyes was as bleak as the sour pasture and no sound, save the cold wind and the silence was fitting for that.

'It was your father? Aye, I suppose, right enough . . .' said the fiddler and he picked up his leather hat. It had salt stains round the brim, brackish as sea lochs and shaped like the seals he'd once played to off the Island of Mull.

9

'What's your name?' asked Martin Farrell as he watched him stoop into shadow under the brim. He was minded to thank him for digging that grave.

'I'm lucky – I've got none,' says the fiddler, and he made no enquiry of Martin's though the lad opened his mouth and told him the same.

'Mine's Farrell. Martin Farrell. I want the Old Man to know.'

'Mother o' Tears!' cried the fiddler. 'What fools ye are on the Border! He's hardly cold in his grave and you're on after following him! And you! A sparrow's egg! Why, lad, stood in bare feet you're not shod in a name! What's a Farrell? Do you know that? Well, do you?'

Martin said nothing, and why ever should he? It was as clear as the day that he was going to be told.

'A rough breed in Ireland and wastrels over here – pocket thieves and chancers, men with no land and seven wives in seven towns, save the ones that make clever with their blue eyes and wed up with some widow to drink off her man's land. Ach, they're like feathers, blowing every which way in the wind.'

'Was that a song for the man I called father?' said Martin. It stung him. 'I don't care for the tune.'

Well, the fiddler felt sorry then. After all, what was left to this lad? He was tired and he thought it a shame. He liked the look of the youth, the still way he stood there next to that grave, with a fresh bruise on his face and a cut on his arm. He thought he'd the look of a woman he'd once played for, but she was a Graham, so how could that be? Oh, away to Hell, he was thinking, this was none of his business (and foul business it was) so why should he care?

Though he, himself, was sore at the Armstrongs. He'd

played fifty fine tunes for them and their dancing and what was the pay? To leave with his life. He was a wise enough man not to argue and to know any road travelled is travelled by steps, but it still made him smart to have been ill-used like that.

So he said it out loud. 'Away to hell, lad! What ever ye have to say to the Old Man you'll need a sharp tongue, and I warrant you've no even a pocket-knife and only ten toes for a horse. Farrell, they call ye?' Then he asked, quieter, 'Was your mother at home?'

'No. She's long dead. Can you lend me a blade?'

It sore vexed the fiddler to have the lad stand there so quiet with old grief and strange courage like a flame in his eyes.

'And what if I gave you one – that is if I had it? Next thing your wee ghost would be back begging for the song of your end! And what should I call it? "The wee fallen sparrow?" '

'Do ghosts ask you such things?' says Martin Farrell.

That made the fiddler touch a tooth with his thumbnail, gnaw off a sliver and spit on the ground.

'Aye. I've known it. Only once, mind. That was enough.' He picked up his fiddle and played four low notes like the howl of a dog and the freezing of blood. 'It's not a song I play often and not one as I could say in all truth that I liked . . . Martin Farrell, leave this alone, lad. You could walk up the road with me a step and a step and there's nothing here in this place need make you look back.'

Turn your head! Let's leave the lad wi' his pride! Those words have sprung tears, the way kindness does when you've known little of it.

The Galloway fiddler waited for Martin under the brim-shadow of his travel-stained hat.

The lad was long to make answer. At last, then, he said, 'Fiddler, I'll go with you. Aye, I'll walk a wee pace till I find the right road to bring me on back.'

'Aye,' said the fiddler. He picked up his pack.

He didn't think anything of the blackness of the shadow which walked by the lad's side. He marked it down to the bright sun if he marked it at all. Only later, when the long afternoon lengthened to dusk up on the high moor, did he see how it walked, tall as a grown man, ahead of the lad on the stony dry track. Tall and striding that shadow, at the feet of Martin Farrell and leading him on. Aye, well, but by then the fiddler had reason to fear night and its allies. He was carrying a dark burden of his own in his pack.

What had he left behind him, the boy? His inheritance? His house and his land? Is that what you think? You must think him a fool.

The bony cow and her calf had been driven off by Jock's Alan – bloody handprints like brands drying hard on their hides. The last bowl of buttermilk had been thrown on the fire in a sputter and stink. Farrell's horse was gone from the stall.

The kist was a nest for a throne of English rats (then it had been for years, since Farrell had hidden it high in the roof tree); their fine dandy brood twirled their whiskers in the moth webs of his mother's once fine Graham lace. They ran collared like courtiers in threads of the same. Ah, it makes you spit on the ground to hear such a thing.

So, away! Away! Let the lad be! Easy enough to walk from that place with the tall Galloway fiddler! You, your proud self, you'd have found it simple enough.

But what of that devil? I mean that black boar – murdering brute – the one with the wee Irish man's blood still wet on its tusks?

The fiddler had butchered it. For all his musical fingers, his loping long legs, he was a brave one and wise in old lore, the tall traveller in his stained hat.

He had been first to the desolate house, first to the sty, thinking bacon, a wee thieving, some runt of a litter he could buckle for a late breakfast in his pack. A hunger like his needed curing. What he'd found was the boar, snoozing in entrails, and the drunk, what was left of him, and two crows perched in an elder above, spelling the beast to go on dreaming so they could finish the meal off.

That had made him put a knuckle to the bile on his teeth, draw a deep breath and wipe his mouth on his sleeve. Then he'd gone to the peat sled and found a sharp slane-spade used for riving out sods.

He had watched off a far island, once, men wading in grey waves among ice, killing whales in a bay encircled by boats. It had taught him the tune of such things – though that was a merry one compared to this. It took thirteen blows to the boar for to kill it. Then he cut out its heart. This organ he tied in a parcel of old sacking and moss. And where has he put it? Look in his pack.

What of the meat? You poor dog! Here's pity on your hunger to ask after hog flesh so tainted!

He'd his own ways, the fiddler, learned on a long path. He did what the day brought and never no more, like a man finding balance crossing a river, making a sure step from stone to greased stone. So take heed how he buried those corpses together, the man's and the hog's in the same grave – for where did Farrell's soul lie when he's misused like that?

The fiddler's a man of high lonely pathways, used to sleeping under a coverlet of stars. He's taken the boar's heart to be sunk at a cross-roads to save all fellow travellers from the haunt of the fetch such a death might raise back. He's to stake it with rowan, a sliver of wood from the true mountain ash, for that way there'd be no chance of a follow from the half-ghost of a peat-cutter with a mouth full of tusks.

Aye, right enough, you can see for our fiddler this day went on all morning, then all afternoon as he strode at Martin's side, and when it came to the evening he'd to face the sun going down. And what was he thinking? Damn this devil road and a curse on the Armstrongs whose sharp lusts set me on it! He'd just too much company for a poet-diviner who most had the good sense to walk his life's path alone.

He had the boy, Martin, stumbling beside him, though

he'd never once stop and never once rest. He'd his fiddle, pegs slackened, to ease back into song, to make everything right with again. And he'd the brute's heart to stake a foul ghost from, without telling the lad. He was a man of that set.

He knew, did the fiddler, he'd but dawn to get the job done by. He could hear two cocks crow, but Tears of Our Lady! Hear a third and the fetch would be free! After that it would take a whole barrel of salt-sober priests with bell, book and candle, to send the tusked horror on its heavenward way. And where was a man to find them in the borders that day?

You might think he was weary, the Galloway fiddler. He was. No man travels lightly but few men travel burdened like that.

Blue dusk was around them when they followed a deer-trod down from the moss, and rooks straggled in silence back to the woods as the pair waded the river in a little known place.

'Away! Can ye suffer these biters?' asked the fiddler, watching the flying things dancing reels over the water. 'If ye can, we'll make a fire here.'

What didn't he say? That he was cold, though it was yet a warm evening, from the chill burden he carried. That there's something holy about fast flowing water. That it would cover the sound – for that pig's heart was still beating. He'd heard it all day, like the blood in the ear of a man who's been running – a sound far, high, and wild like an Irish bone drum.

They climbed up from the reeds and the mist and the bushes to a small rocky place where the midges were less. There they got a flame kindled and sat close by that.

It was summer, too light for a flame, but each thing draws its opposite. Fire made that dusk dark.

Martin watched as the fiddler humped off his pack. Wolf-hunger shone green in his motherless eyes. 'Did you play at the wedding?' said the quiet lad.

'Hah!' cried the fiddler. 'I've nothing to give ye! I saw dainties consumed with a knife at my throat. Pike steaks stuffed with cress on a bed of white lilies, squirrels hoarded with nuts and glazed with wild honey, and snipe wrapped around bilberry jelly in little speared tarts with their long beaks through their breasts . . .'

'Is that truth?' asked Martin, his knees cleaved to his belly. Hunger the egg he hatched in his throat.

'No. It's not,' said the fiddler. 'There was burnt beef and porridge. But you asked for a tune, lad, so I played that cruel note. Now hark to my words. I've nothing to give you – fill your belly with river or else it must yawn.'

Martin was silent. He watched the sticks burn.

Away to Hell! thought the fiddler, running his thumb down the gristly bone that made his long nose. He squinted at Martin, rubbing his chin with the heel of his thumb. 'Martin Farrell, where were ye when they brought your father home?'

What can Martin tell him? Of a stranger, dressed in stinking black tatters, who galloped him by moonlight all the way to the dawn? He tells it. The truth, as he knows it. And our Galloway man? He's quick to take hold of the tune.

The fiddler listened in silence, then picked up his fiddle and twisted a peg. He plucked a low note with his thumb. 'I know that man,' he says with a frown. 'Did he speak to ye, lad?'

'Aye, he did,' says the boy. 'He said that the crow had robbed a strange nest.'

Our Galloway man barked a sharp laugh. 'Aye! It's Neb Corbie who's put ye in debt for your life!'

'Neb Corbie? What's his business wi' me?' says the lad.

'Some call him Wull O' The Shroud, some Dead O' Night, but most call him Neb Corbie . . . His business? Ask the carrion crow who sits in the thorn tree with his beak to the wind! Neb Corbie's a fellow of the same scavenging guild. Don't ye know of him? His art? It's to spy and to tell. He can reckon the price some fool wedded man will pay for a lady's kerchief he's found in the whins when *her* husband's in Berwick! There's no man secretly poisoned or stabbed on the moss, no new-born babe buried under a bush, no doing, no matter how secret, he'll not set his black nose to and sniff the gold to be got.'

Martin watched a coil of green smoke hiss from a damp stick. 'Yet, he saved my skin, fiddler . . .'

The fiddler shrugged his lean shoulders. 'Then he's a mind to invest in the tale of a peat-cutter's lad that he's dragged from harm's reach. Why? I can't tell ye. He walks his own path.'

'Should I fear him?' asked Martin. (Do you think him a coward? I call him wise lad.)

'Fear him?' Again came the shrug. 'Neb Corbie? If you've secrets you'll fear him like fire,' says the fiddler, watching the boy's face but he saw not a flinch. 'If ye have none? To Hell! He's a stout man to drink with, quick with a jest and a great bell of a laugh. There's many a hovel where the Crow of the Border is a glad welcome guest. He comes with his flask. And if he takes away gossip? What of it? Who cares? Not the wife who finds a coin in her milking bowl or else in the ashes when she stirs them at dawn! No, Martin Farrell, truth being truth, it's easy to tell – those who fear Neb Corbie already fear Hell . . .'

And thinking of such, the fiddler saw how the stars had pricked into place and bade Martin sleep. He watched him lie down, and played a sweet tune on his fiddle until the youth slept. Then he set it aside and waited for the slumber of the long steady breath.

The fiddler blinked off his own sleep, stroked his fiddle's worn breast. He heard the pig's heart drum-drumming as the wings of the night spread their silence like the quartering white owl.

A long time, he waited. Then he stood. His knees creaked.

And Martin Farrell drew up on one elbow, out of his sleep. 'It's not for my hunger I ask it,' said the lad's voice all drowsy, 'but fiddler, what can ye give that woman yonder begging for the ham in your pack? It's to feed her wee bairn.'

What woman? What bairn? It made the tall man's teeth click together! He watched Martin sink back to dreams and dark slumber before risking a glimpse over his left shoulder to see.

And what was there there? A fox, could it be? In the roots of a hawthorn? A shadow tangled by flames in the rowan's soft sway? Whatever was watching under yon tree, it was no Christian woman begging for his charity.

'Sleep,' hushed the fiddler, touching Martin's cool brow. 'Say the prayers your poor mother taught ye to keep us safe till dawn.'

The fire died down. The fiddler sat with his back to a stone. It seemed the boy slept, so he rose with the boar's heart and crept softly away. But he's taken three steps when he hears Martin cry, 'Fiddler, for pity, give that ham in your pack to yon woman. Her bairn will die!'

'Sleep,' said the fiddler, down on his hunkers, he could feel the hairs on his head prickling to white. But Martin *was* sleeping, all loose-limbed and easy as if neither ghosts nor dank grief had their place in the night.

The fiddler crouched and he waited, feeling the muscular ghost of that fetch strive to be free. And he waited as the first breath of the dawn wind stirred in the grasses, moved the leaves of the rowan tree. Then he stood, broke off a stick, and his own heart was thundering now as loud as the boar's. He's taken seven steps when he hears Martin cry, 'Fiddler! Love of Heaven! Give that ham to the beggar, else she'll kill her own babe to save it dying this way!'

Our fiddler! He knelt, wretched, then grabbed up his fiddle bow all made of the horse tails, the white hair and the grey, and he held the boy's head to his shoulder, like the music he cradled, and drew the bow gently across Martin's young lips. 'Hush,' he said. 'Whisht . . . You'll hear nothing, say nothing, till my next note sets ye free . . .' Then he let the boy lie.

Only the dawn star was left in the sky.

Martin Farrell slid down into a fathom of silence, in company there with the quiet fiddle which lay wrapped in a cloth. For a child with no family, no parents, no kin, that dawn he was bedded with the pitch-note of music, aye, silence, for his twin.

Is it true what I tell you? It's what I've heard say. How the fiddler fled like a man before fire as the blush of the new light came to the sky. What befell him? Hold your tongue and I'll tell!

Our man scrambled among rushes and whins to the peat

bog and heather and all manner of creatures buzzed up in his path. The gadders. The biters. The cleggs with yellow faces that drive cattle mad. Below him, the river seethed like a cauldron with the trout breaking fast. Still, on ran the fiddler, flicking a hand to clear a path for his face, until he stood at the rise, saw the roads, how they ran like two ribbons in the hair of the moors till they touched and were tied, and there was the cross. He sighed, took a breath. The safe grave for the fetch was but thirty steps off.

He took the first stride, treading wary, finding a tussock to keep out of the bog. His boot sank in brown water – such a step robbed his breath! But it held. He came to no harm. With a laugh he jumped to another.

Then up rose the swarm.

Out of bog-reed and peat-soak, it rushed, as if each flying thing on the earth had suddenly hatched. Glittering flies with out-riders of midges swirled up in a black glint of wings, higher and higher, tall as the ghost of a man in chain-mail.

What was it? Some fetch born of maggots challenging his path? Some fetch come to set the tusked peat-cutter free?

What could he do? Faced with dreams in his life, the Galloway fiddler was a man to open his eyes and step free. He jumped on towards it. It clashed and kept coming with the *zzzz* of a whetstone being drawn down a blade.

Did that stop him? Though through all the shiver of wings he could still see the road – aye, tell the truth. It did. Wouldn't it ye?

He heard his fear say, 'Drop the swine's heart here! Who could blame ye? Drop it and flee!'

But what stopped the fiddler from running was this. A boy and a fiddle lay ensorcelled in silence and no hand could rouse them back to the tune of themselves, save only his.

So he gave a great cry and ran at the swarm, leaping step after step, till he passed through its midst. It cloaked him! His shirt sleeves grew studded with sapphires, his cuffs sprang a black lace. He'd a beard where he grew none as they clung to his face. And where was the sun? A last fingernail tip beneath the east's rim.

'I could leave ye! I could leave ye! Bit o' wood that I whistle on! Child wi' no house! Who would blame me! Ah God!' He cried over, 'Ah God!' and 'Ah God!' as the swarm with its shudder of crawlers ran on his shoulders and cockroached his head.

Now the weight's crushed him down till he's crawling. It's no way to be dying. Soon, he's not spitting curses as he labours, but each pest from his mouth. What's left through the mist-vision of wings? A glimpse of his sweat. In front of his eyes, each drop falls like amber, holding a fly. He scrabbles with fingers to claw his way to the crossroad.

And the sun? Whisht! Hold your breath! It rises each dawn and never no matter that this be the day of your birth or the day of your death.

Where else was dawn breaking? Over the whole land, ye daftie! Didn't you know that? Oh, I'll give you the notion each child, man and woman gets to thinking the sun's only risen on them. It takes a traveller, a sailor, or a rare kind of cleric to disabuse them of that!

So it rose on the Armstrongs, though not all Armstrongs rose. There had been a great wedding. Some were still, the night after, sleeping it off. Will Armstrong was roused, though he pretended to doze, watching his new wife wash her body at an earthenware bowl. He didn't let her finish her lovely ablutions, but would use his rough fingers to comb out her long hair.

There was a clatter of hooves in the courtyard as the Old Man rode in with his flank troop of jack-coats. He watched them dismount in the silence of servants asleep and wedding-guests gone. He watched them tie the fierce sleugh-hounds to the iron ring in the wall, lead their mud-shaggy horses to water and straw in the stall. Now, quite alone, he smells the dawn breeze, cool and damp off the moor-moss, then opens one eye and looks up at the tower where the voice of Anne Eliot flies from the window like Noah's white dove.

But his is a dangerous squint, for he's one eye on the bony brown cattle someone's tethered like a dowry at the door of his hall. A skinny cow and a calf. He touches his teeth with his tongue as he reckons the brand. A bloody handprint. Oh yes, black and dry as it was, the hide-hairs clagged together, the Old Man knew from his own ridings exactly what manner of barter fashioned markings like those.

See how her flank shudders as his gaze touches upon her, as he studies the wee notch in her hoof. Jock's Alan? He'd been too drunk to see it when he drove the beasts down. Were they Farrell's cattle?

Ask the Old Man who'd made him that loan.

When his steward came to greet him he saw how the Old Man appeared in rapt contemplation to be watching a cloud like a feather above the tower wall, with an eye as red as an eclipse of the moon.

Someone was dying who didn't yet know it. Someone asleep. Someone who'd taken the edge off their drinking with a galloping ride and a little light killing for the bride's sake. Someone who seemed to have forgotten that this business of vengeance could, after all, affect a man's health.

'Am I wanted?' asked the steward. A quease in his belly made him belch a sour breath.

The Old Man glanced at the cattle, then inspected the crook nail on his old yellow thumb. 'The laddie who brought these?'

'He's only just woken.'

'A shame,' said the Old Man. 'I'd prefer him to sleep.'

By the time that the sun was high enough to cast shadows, Jock's Alan was dead.

'It's a shame,' said the steward, when he came back. 'That cousin of fair Anne's has been found in the river. He must have gone to make water when he was swilled up with drink.'

'Convey to the Eliots my magnanimous sorrow,' said the Old Man. 'Now ask your wife for fresh linen. Your breeches are wet.'

Oh, what a sweet morning in the peaceable Border! Up on the moors the day's green shot and golden as silk from the East. The larks' voices, what are they like? Like standing under the freshest of waterfalls and climbing the thirst quench of each falling drop.

In the tower, at the archer's slit window, Anne Eliot, newly married, could have sponged her bare skin with the day, plunged like a salmon into the clear air!

Lovely child. Lovely and cool, she lets her shift slide down over her shoulders, sets the thinnest of gold chains to slip on her throat. She thinks this a new life – a fine one! Not like the old one where her mother could call her to task, saying, 'Get away to your bed!' and 'Don't skrem up your face!' and 'I'll be glad when you're wed, ye keen bitch!'

'Will,' she says. 'Will.'

Was that a question?

'Aye,' comes the answer so we'll suppose that it was.

'Will, come to the window. What do you see?'

He came and stood by her, kissed the bone of her shoulder and the hem of her collar down where her breast dipped.

'You and I,' she said soft, like a seed in his beard, 'We could bring peace to this place.'

His answer? Sharp silence. His body went hard and he held her away. 'And I'd push the wood plough like a farmer?' His mouth twisted. 'Ye soft wench. Get yourself dressed.'

Was that a rebuff? When he stamped from the chamber, she touched her cheek with her hand as if she'd been slapped, so we'll suppose that it was.

Was it *that* set her greeting? She was, after all, an Eliot lass. She should have known better than to speak out so daft. No. It was the sight of Jock's Alan, her favourite cousin, slung over a pack-horse, his head dangling down. His face was as blue as an eel's back and water and blood gushed from his mouth.

'Seems the lad drowned,' said the Armstrongs. Some even believed it. The Eliots? Let's just say they felt a bit strain on their truce with the Old Man that day.

24

As for Anne, she knew that her cousin could swim like a trout, but what could she say? She went back to her chamber and stood quiet as the morning. This was her new life? Then the walls of the tower seemed thick as a dungeon and the thin gold at her throat? Heavy as chains.

What a peaceable sun-rise, ripening with secrets! Under the rowan, Martin Farrell lies sleeping in the shade the leaves cast upon his still face . . .

ire! Fire! Get out of the house! Save the bairns from their beds! Don't open the doors! Don't fan the flames!

Ah, sit back on your arse bones. It was just an alarm to keep ye awake! When it's quiet in the Border there's something amiss. Besides, I've a bit word for you. Are you roused? Are you listening? Then I'm not wasting my breath.

What wrecks a man in a way that destroys him? Do you know that? Cold steel at his throat or forced between teeth? Swallowing minnows and weeds in a river till the last glimpse of his killer goes wavy then blurs?

No. I'd not say so. Those are quick ways of parting. Ask the old whose hands begin shaking as they reach to greet Death.

No. Listen. What does for the most of us — wrecks the soul in its singing of life — is the flies.

You want me to tell of riding and reiving, of fire, feud and dawn raids? Of heroic stands in the river? Men battling it out with the great Jedburgh axe? Then Ho-hoa! Rein in your horses! Pin back your lugs while I speak of the flies.

It starts with the one. You can't sleep for its buzzing. It whines in your ear when ye close both your eyes. Wake, and it settles. Sleep, and it batters the bed-head, gads at the walls.

This new bride, Anne Eliot, has got one. She thought her mother a stinger. That made her glad to run into Will Armstrong's arms. But what's this in her chamber that keeps her from sleeping? Is it, *Get yourself dressed!* or *It seems the lad drowned?*

And the Widow, Margaret Graham, can't comb her grey hair at her mirror for glancing about. She walks from her chair to her window, stands and looks out. She brushes the fly from her cheek with a crow's coal black feather for which she's paid a good price.

And the Old Man? He greets Will Armstrong, his heir, with scarcely a nod. No. He sits with a bannock before him, uneaten from breakfast, and scratches his ear-lobe with his horn yellow thumb.

And what's tickling his thoughts?

'This trouble at the river?' asks Will.

Oh no. Just some private wee matter that concerns nothing more than a peat-cutter's stepson.

All that day and some after, the Old Man flicks at a thought that won't settle, till his mood fills all in the tower with a quarrel like wasps in a bag.

Aye, as I told ye, the test of my sermon is the place of the flies! One's a rare nuisance, three in a chamber can keep a Christian from sleeping, unless he's a born snorer then they'll walk on his lip. Ten round your hat and it's blamed pestilential! But if they keep coming — eleven, twelve, thirteen hundred, then we've to be thinking like camels and that last light straw (aye, in all probability carrying this wee devil awashing its whiskers) that broke the beast's back.

Ask the Galloway fiddler to wax further philosophical on the weight of this pest. But you'd best choose your moment or you might end your enquiry with his fist in your mouth and you spitting teeth.

On this rare lovely morning he was crushed like a man being pressed under stones. Aye, let's go a bit back. On his hands and his knees he crawls to the crossroads and the devils keep swarming to add to his pack.

If you'd seen him there? What? What? What would you have seen? A black sizzing thing, a horrible shadow that crept over the ground. Yet it chants like a hermit! The Galloway fiddler, crushed beyond bearing, is remembering prayers.

Then he sees one last gadder through the veiled vision of wings – its dagger-point face and its bramble-black eyes – and he knows, like the camel (or was it a mule?) if it lands it will kill him! It hums and it hovers in front of his eyes.

'Harrgh!' he breathes. 'Hheww . . .' He blows at the little light demon with what seems, after all, like his very last breath. He stretches his hand, gloved in buzzing black armour, to hold out the boar's heart to the cross of the road.

Was he saved? Shall we ask him?

'Harrgh! Hheww! Fffff . . .' is all he says on the matter, when through the weight and the tickle of legs, feelers and wings, he sees a man's boot! A scuffed toe in brown leather. Mother of love!

He would kiss it, if his mouth wasn't beset by a brank of these flies.

What he hears isn't helpful, above the pests' whine.

'Curse o' the lepers! Kick this carrion off the highway! Make clean the path!'

The fiddler? He saw the boot swinging, saw the soil dust it lifted when raised. He took the blow on his shoulder. It near broke the bone.

But now here's his delight! For one breath of a moment it unsettled the swarm! With a wild grunt he's forward in the midst of the crossroad as he's suddenly lit by the sun's first bright rays.

Let's not forget, in the whoop of his joy he finds himself hugging an unfriendly leg.

And the flies? Remember those swine that some demon fled into? How they crashed from a cliff? With a scream like a hog killed, the swarm spun away. The wind from their wings tore the shirt from one rider, another's horse bolted, and a sealed English warrant giving legal grant to pursuers of Armstrongs was shredded like snow and whirled in a blizzard to settle on some drovers over Bewcastle way.

Stripped of the flies, the Galloway fiddler found his shape as a man. He knelt on his knees, pulled the hat from his head and punched a hailstorm of wing-glitter out from its brim. He looked at the boot then up into the red whiskers and foul teeth of the fellow who wore it. But for thanks he had neither the voice nor the time.

Six riders in jack-coats, mail stitched on leather, hands on their pike shafts, watched in a ring as the Galloway fiddler scuttled a hole in the earth like a dog, shoved the boar's heart within. Then with the stick from the rowan he jabbed it to rest. With scarce strength in his finger bones he scrabbed the soil back to give Farrell's fetch its earned peace.

Then he was done. Here was the dawn. Here the warm sun. The fiddler might have fallen, stretched on his face, but where in that thistle of weapons was a man to lie down?

'Did I see that? Did my eyes tell me true?' asked a proud man on horseback. He wore a gold ring.

'Aye,' said the fellow in boots. 'Aye, Hughie Graham. Like men who shared the one bottle, we all saw the same thing.'

There was silence. High over the crossroads a lark rose up singing like a soul that's set free. The horses grew shadows. The Galloway fiddler cleared the stubble of fly legs from his cheeks and his chin.

'Ahh,' says the stranger, squinting all twisted down from his horse. 'Now I ken who ye are! I hear ye played a fine reel at a wedding not but two nights just passed! What have ye buried?'

'A piece of green bacon,' answered the fiddler. 'Read the prophets and Jews for their warning on that.'

Was the fiddler in danger? Hughie Graham's cold smile could well be your answer. His black eyes searched the shade under our Galloway man's hat.

'Has fate crossed us?' asked the fiddler.

'Aye, man,' answers Hughie, 'it seems that it has. It's a wee lad we're after . . . Ah! By your blink and your flinch, I'd say you know where he is! That's good, tuneful friend. That's good. He's a kinsman of my great-aunt, Margaret Graham. He'll come to no harm riding wi' us . . .'

What was our man to answer? He's left Martin sleeping in a spelled silent dream and he knows nothing will rouse him till he plays him a tune. Not crows on his shoulders nor picking his bones. But, Martin Farrell — a *Graham*? The fiddler fingered a notion to let the boy slumber forever like a stone on the hill. Was that worse than to wake him to a place in black feud? But away to Hell, it was none of his business! Why should he care? The lad, like the rest of us, was shod in his fate!

Besides, six pikes pricked his wind-box to help him find a voice. 'Aye,' he says quietly. 'I know where he is. That bacon I buried was a cure for his mind.'

When he heard that, Hughie Graham, the Widow's great-nephew, smiled a bit smile, showing each sharp yellow tooth just like a stoat.

What had he done? After all, these are kinsfolk. Hah! Let me tell ye the truth. Five are plain ruffians and scoundrels, aye, wolfheads and outlaws made up Hughie's troop.

He'll come to no harm riding wi' us . . . Did the fiddler believe that? He tells himself, 'Aye'. But there's a pain in his liver, his bladder, his bones which keeps grumbling 'Nay'. As he led them to Martin he watched how clouds from the North rose to cover the sun.

'The lad sleeps off a fever,' he said, as the strangers stood round him under the rowan where Martin lay. He picked up his fiddle, but held it quite silent. He can no find the heart to waken the lad into this darkening day.

'Ye'll ride with us,' says Hughie.

'I will?' says the fiddler.

'You will,' says Hughie Graham. 'Either tied to the saddle or wi' your hands free. My great-aunt is old, withered, vexatious, so ye might spend our long ride, fiddler, choosing some tune ye might play . . .'

By noon the sky's black and blue-black are the mountains jagged up by lightning as it cracks far away. Martin Farrell? He's slung over a pack-horse, his old shirt slipping down off his shoulders while the cold slanting rain runs off his bare back. Still under the bow's spell, our lad sleeps on. He doesn't feel how the crown hair of his head dangles in water as they ford a fast stream nor hear the crash of the thunder above a forest of pines.

The tall fiddler rides silent, clinging with flayed fingers to the reins of his mount. His eyes? They're as grey as the storm cloud under the rain-blackened brim of his hat. What is he thinking?

A curse on this path! But what can he do? He remembers a time, when lost in a mist, he'd sat on his back side and starved for three days until it had passed. When it cleared? He'd found himself looking out over the sea from the edge of a cliff.

At last, in the glant of the lightning he sees a dark tower. He looks at the lad and reaches for the fiddle beneath his drenched coat.

As they rode down, Hughie Graham snarled at the

fiddler, 'Christ! Do ye call that a tune! If you'll not play for the Grahams as ye played for the Armstrongs, then I know a sure way to teach ye to sing!' Then he leered closer. 'Nay, peace on ye, fiddler . . . What did ye bury up there at the crossroads?'

'The heart of the pig that ate the heart of a man. If it's treasure you're after, Hughie Graham, now you know where to dig.'

The Widow's great-nephew whipped up his horse and rode full of fury in through the gate. The Galloway man? He gave a bit smile, just a wee hook of a grin at the edge of his lip. He knew he'd made a straight strike. He'd guessed Hughie's game. A landless great-nephew paying court to the Widow, and all her sons dead! It was a dangerous pleasure to relish his hit, but he did.

They were led into the courtyard with its hens and its dogs. And that's where the lad woke, brought back to himself by the fiddler's strange notes.

Aye, he woke in a bafflement, dangling over mud brogged deep with hoofprints, still tied to a pack-horse that stood bogged in mire at the foot of a tower. 'God's Nails! Where are we?'

The fiddler dismounted beside him and tugged loose Martin's ropes. He helped the lad stand. 'Rub the blood back to your wrists, lad. We're in a dark place.'

But he stilled the boy's gasp with a breath on his finger. Hughie Graham was back, booting hens from the threshold and pushing open the door.

In her chamber, the Widow hears the riders come in. The great gate squeals shut. The crossbolts slam home. Does she go to her window?

No. As the dusk darkens, she sits by a candle, watching a spider spinning a web. Her knuckles are white. Love? In this dark tower, it's a knot in a cord then a blade of cold steel cutting it through.

Knotting and binding, the old arts of tying – to take a child from the womb or lower a coffin in a grave with two ropes. Is that witchcraft? In this place, in these debatable years, it was a woman's high art.

Margaret Graham, steeped in grief for a daughter despoiled by an Armstrong, for four sons and her man, murdered by Armstrongs, she was more skilled than most.

She glanced up from her reverie as Hughie opened the door. She turned from the web and unclenched her fist. With a soft giddy flutter a small fly reeled from her palm. Or was it a moth? It flew direct through the candle flame in a cindering flare.

'Great-aunt? The lad you were seeking. He's here.'

So then, our lad, Martin Farrell, he sat on a bench in the Widow's dark hall. Rain dripped from his hair, his breeks, his soaked shirt, and a sunk bellied greyhound lapped from the puddle that spread at his heel.

Bruised from the riding and daft from his dreams, he stared into the blue flame of a candle that stood on the board.

Did he mourn the wee man? Aye, tell the truth. Aye, he did. For the first time in his lived life he sat on a good oak bench by a hearth of cut stones, yet he yearned for a grim hand to drag him back home. A snarl of 'Get up off yer arse! Get the fire lit!' The slapping thud of a hare slung at his feet to joint for the pot.

Mourn the devil ye know! Ye'll not let him rest. The lad yearned for Farrell's foul breath, his tannery stink, the deep lines by his nose, etched brown with the peat.

Away, Martin Farrell! Where are ye? Who are ye? That ye mourn this fool ye much feared? Whisht . . . We torment him with questions, an inquisition of doubts. Let him blink at the flame.

The Galloway fiddler? He's there at his side, wringing out his drowned hat. Martin hears the drops splash, sees them burst like fat roses as they hit the hard flags.

That shook him awake. The dog snuffed from his feet to this new crimson pool.

'Fiddler?' he gasped. He grabbed the man's hand and turned it palm up. What did he see – a lifeline like a river fed from fine streams of blood. Our Galloway man's palm was raw to the bone from his morning's work.

Some say that the lad was startled to tears which fell on the sores – a miracle balm which made the flesh whole.

Soft folks with soft notions murder the truth. There are six kinds of men who fear the loss of their hands. The lover of ladies, for reasons ye'll guess. The swordsman with a delicate, murderous grasp. The miser stumped from his palming of gold. The pickpocket who'd starve if he lost his light touch. The small man with his children at the gate of his field. And the sixth? Aye, a fine fiddler. Ours was one of the best.

So he snatched back his hand and with a snarl passed the palm through the flame of the candle close by Martin's face. His jaw clicked in a grimace, then he huffed a deep breath and smiled at the lad.

'Who are ye?' whispered Martin.

'I could ask ye the same,' answered the fiddler. Outside, the storm broke. The thunder left silence. In the woods a bird sang. And over the board five midges made a small bouncing dance. With the patience of Job, the fiddler swiped them away with a waft of his hat.

It was then Hughie Graham came back into the hall with a crookety servant carrying a flagon of wine. Aye, it's the stoat with an entourage of one elderly dog! (Ah, forgive me, forgive me, all you landless, ambitious, flattering, treacherous men as take sides with Hughie, for so partial a portrait!)

Elaborate, devious as the whole English Court, he bade his guests welcome! Bade them both sup! His great-aunt was at prayer but would come down and join them on her solemn, 'Amen'. Pious Widow. So be at their ease. (Where was his troop? Don't ask. Ye'll regret it. As did the lass.)

Aye, Hughie Graham . . . Drink! he cries. Sup! The smile on his lips never honeyed his eyes. They were as yellow as poison as he raised his cup to the child.

But he smiled. See the stoat smile . . . Watch him, Martin Farrell. See how he raises his cup in a toast then watches you drink, like a man contemplating garrotting, pressing the brim to his throat. It's a smile like a knife. There's many a scream flown to its point.

Oh, Hughie Graham, he played the good host. More wine! More wood on the fire! A man with very clean hands. Given to washing and wearing lace at his sleeves. His thoughts? Byzantine. When they dwell upon Death, it's never his own . . .

'It's a marvellous chance that I should find distant kin I thought lost!' cries Hughie.

Does the lad answer? His mouth's swilled with wine? Has it robbed him of sense? Ye fools! He's a creature of moors and the wide high peat bog. What has he learnt from the hare? How she crouches. The lapwing? The grouse on her nest? The adder? The lark?

The fiddler spoke for him. The only man there now who seemed at his ease.

With the pouring of wine, he'd stretched out his long legs, quaffed deep from his cup, wiped his lips on his sleeve, then crankled his foot bones to the toes of his boots till they settled in comfort. His hat (aye, it was drying . . .) raked a shadow over one eye. His mouth hooked in a grin. It seems he's vastly amused by some secret jest.

Hughie Graham guessed, rightly, that it was at his expense.

'Kin?' mused the fiddler. 'It's well we might be. For we share much in common – an inheritance of air, the bequest of a road . . .'

Hughie Graham was needled. 'You're bold for a beggar! I spoke to the child.'

'Aye,' said the fiddler. 'Very bold are the fellows who have nothing to lose. Shall we debate that philosophy?' He glanced sideways at Martin. 'What say ye, *child*?'

Hughie's smile never changed. Aye, but it seems that he suffers the torments of toothache . . . 'All men have something they guard, fiddler. And well ye know it. I can see you're no fool.'

Our Galloway man? He lifted one shoulder. (Shall we forgive him the raw hand he has pressed 'tween his knees?) He let it drop, and then said, 'For a man who has nothing, only *want* can be lost. Would ye not say so? And a man without wants – why, he's free as a bird!'

Was that a laugh? That sound like the splintering of midwinter ice? It came from the stoat. We'll suppose that it was. Most charming. Quite false. 'Eloquent beggar, with holes in your boots. What wants are yours?'

'To see what the day brings. Enter night when it comes. Master Graham, speaking plain truth, don't ye find that enough?'

Was their host in agreement? I'll leave ye to judge.

With an icicle smile Hughie called for more wine.

'Fiddler,' said our quiet lad, 'whoever ye be. I'm glad I sit at your side. That I have ye to trust.'

'Trust!' the Galloway man hissed. His face seemed half mortal, half shadow, beneath his hat's brim. 'On your road, Martin Farrell, trust only one man.'

'God's Truth! Fiddler, who is he?'

Across the wide table, Hughie Graham's ears – defying anatomy – turned to their breeze.

The fiddler's silence? Away! It's a sermon on riddles. He's to make it a short one as they wait for the Widow. That's her tread on the stairs!

What do they tell of that meeting? How at the door of the stairwell which wound up to the tower, a vivid brand flared?

Shadows reared on the flagstones and the skirl of a drum filled all the hall?

Incredulous fools! The din and the drum? Shall I tell what they were? Why, nothing more than the crookety servant dragging a box *clump clump* down the steps! Aye, a stout kist, hinged, edged, angled and flanked with forged iron and made fast with a devilish lock.

Wee crookety man. That box bends him quite double, bangs his brittle shin-pans. It's woe to his wedding tackle to be humping the weight across to the hearth.

Hughie Graham's teeth clipped on his cup. For most of his years he's been hunting the key for the keek in that chest.

Martin Farrell, from the dragging of peat-sleds, felt the strain of the load. He stepped from the bench to help the old crither lower his end. Was he thanked for his trouble?

The servant spat bile. 'Bairn,' he hissed through his last seven teeth. 'Would ye steal mi' endeavour when it's all I have left!'

The wise lad stepped back, then he glanced at the fiddler. The Galloway man stood with his hat in his hands, had uncovered his head.

The fiddler said, 'Lady . . .'

The Widow said, 'Fiddler, is my wine good?'

'Aye, Mistress Graham, aye, that it is.'

Was she old, cold and stately? Or mad as the North Wind gone icy with grief? Ach, pass me the jug! Aye, give me a sup. The bairns are asleep. Ease their wee heads from the snug of your knee, your quiet arm's crook, and come to the door. Breathe the night's sober chill.

There's no wind at all. Just the line of the moors, the dark of the moss, a pricking of stars by the high Hangin Stones.

On this most moonless of nights, where is the moon? Ask the salmon asleep in the deep river pool.

Do ye fear the night? Will ye have your bairns sleep? Ach, you're wanting a tale, not the truth about love!

The fiddler knows what he saw. Let that be enough. The peat-cutter's stepson found himself judged by a pair of clear eyes under raven black brows. Poor lapwing's egg! He's no manners as such. His heart knocks in his throat as he stands by the box.

The crookety servant thrust a log on the fire. Martin's shadow – aye, Margaret Graham saw it – lifted its head to the roof-tree as it rose up the wall.

With a fine courtly flourish, Hughie Graham brought her to the chair. But what's the stoat gained? A fine wagging tail. What has he lost? Ask the cur.

'Martin o' the Foul-bog Syke,' the Widow said. 'I've brought ye here at last.'

Poor peat-cutter's stepson! His heart is a moth!

'What have ye of your mother?' the lady asked.

There's a bit hesitation? Away! His heart's stopped! It won't beat again till he pulls the pouch from his shirt and pours the smallest of finger rings into his fist.

'This.' A ring, such a little thing, twiddled with letters.

Where is the fiddler? A shadow standing in shadows. Hughie Graham? Ah, like the chief guest at his funeral he's the face the bit green. They watch as the Widow stretches her hand to show the beggarly lad the twin of that circle on her own right hand.

Lover's candle, tide-chart of wombs, murder's accomplice, the moon, they say that it showed its face at the high archer's window as Martin asked softly, 'Lady, are we kin?'

'I gave birth to Bess Graham. Did she give birth to thee?'

'Wounds o' God! Madam!' cried Hughie Graham, 'do I ken that you claim him? Do you name him for yours? This, this *abortion*!'

Margaret Graham rose. A small woman, yet she towered like a tree. Her glare stopped the man's blether. Martin sank to his knees by the great iron-bound kist. For all the sleeping he's done, he finds himself tired. In need of a rest. He stares at the Widow like a starveling bairn. What does she give him, Margaret Graham? Her face is all bone.

'Is it *Graham*, ye call me?' he whispered. 'Of your house and your line?'

'If ye can open the kist ye'll have what ye own.'

It's a gift from his grandam? He heaves at the lid and the silence is filled with the huff of his breath. Where is the key?

'Mother of mercy! Where is the key?' Martin cries out at last.

Margaret Graham, she smiled. 'You'll find it to hand.' And with that he's dismissed. 'Fetch flesh and salt bread for our supper,' she called to the servant. 'Fiddler, what will ye play to earn your night's crust?'

Our Galloway man, does he protest he'd no chosen to come to this place, or show her his raw palms still seeping with blood? Away! Away! He's put on his hat and watches the lad from the shadow beneath and he's glanced at the stoat, Hughie Graham, seen how his eyes have turned to the smallest of slits, like the small wounds a knife makes when thrust in a back. Away to Hell, he was thinking, let the Old Villain take who He will, but it'll no be for trying!

He caught up his fiddle, though she's all out of tune, tapped his bow on his thigh, cried, 'Lady! I'll play a fine reel! In all modest truth, it's one of my own!'

And with that he set to with a terrible skreal, no note that rang true! A murder of tom-cats! A garrotting of hares!

See Hughie Graham. He kicked back his chair, snatched the knife from his belt. Insult! Aye, insult it was! A torment to the ears. But they say that the Widow bade the stoat sit, sipped wine from her cup. She was old. Was she deaf? I'd not say so. She smiled her dark smile.

And our peat-cutter's stepson? He first stood his ground in the shriek of that gale. He'd know something like it in his life on the moss. Aye, and it could be true, the fiddler was playing the storm of his thoughts.

The Galloway man whirls, stamps his foot, and still he plays on. His eyes glitter in blackness beneath his hat's brim in this tune of a screech owl ripped wing from wing.

Watch Martin Farrell in the howl of that din. His body is shaking. He sees the fiddler's blood ribbon his wrists, swirl from his elbows and splatter the floor, and he thrusts his two fingers into his ears. At last, he cries, 'Christ! Mother of Mercy! Christ! Fiddler, stop!'

Silence rang in the hall. The fiddler swayed on his heels, yet he still had the strength to give the bit grin, bow deep to the Widow and sweep off his hat.

'Fiddler,' whispered Martin. 'What do ye call that?'

'Hah!' croaked the fiddler. He lurched to the table and with a slippery hand picked up his cup. He gulped down the wine and reached for the jug. Sweat crowned his brow, his lips were gone grey. 'Can ye no guess? It's all played in one key.'

What did he say? Martin must read his mouth, for, if it's hearing he's after then his two grubby digits still block the passage that way!

In that thundering silence he turned from the fiddler and

stared at the kist. *The key is to hand.* What had he learned from the man he'd called father, Farrell, the chancer? Martin lowered his hands, knelt by the box and thrust his wee finger into the keyhole. *Tack-clack. Clack-tack.* He turned it once to the sinister, once to the dexter. All in the hall heard the lock spring with a click.

Is it true? Ye ask it? Away! You want the tale's end? Then hold your tongue's clatter, keep faith wi' the tale!

Whisht! Even foul Hughie Graham was snared by the quiet. Ach, ye must wait. My bladder is full. Open the door, let me into the yard. I'll piss like the cattle under the stars . . . Ah, a man's lighter for that! Here, sniff my boot . . . Nay, I'll do it for ye! Take a deep huff . . . It's the loveliest whiff, the scent of the loam, the damp loam and the green spike of the hyacinth that stirs beneath ice. Snowdrop and wormcast, the rotting oak leaf, the deep churn of the peat beneath the hardest hoar frost. Away. My boot's on the floor. Leave that to the poets. Pass me the jug.

So then, Martin kneels by the kist. Does he open the lid? In the quiet of the hall, our lad's rested his elbows on the black wood, pressed knuckle to teeth. Why? Do ye ask it? Because he's afeared! Aye, mortal terror is what you behold. Have you never felt it? Are ye cowards or sleepwalkers? Ach, ye poor fools. Fear is the door ye have to pass through if you will wake up!

What was he thinking, this peat-cutter's lad? He'd the bit notion his destiny was shut in that kist. Aye, in his terror he grasped that *chance* was a dice game men blindly play, but that game wasn't his.

Hughie Graham? Hah, he's half throttled from biting the air and grinding his teeth. The crookety servant seemed in fear of his life. He cringed like a dog. What of it? He was that make of man. A post to be whipped.

Outside, in the moonlight on the wide blue moors a horseman stood motionless in black silhouette. In each deep river pool the moon rose like a breast. A vixen pissed musk on the whins, adjusted her mask. The tawny owl swivelled a blink. In Anne Eliot's womb it seemed drowning fingers reached up for help.

At last, Hughie croaked like a raven. 'Open it! Open it!'

The fiddler laughed. And, as if he awoke, Martin raised up the lid.

Hughie saw moonlight on silver and groaned at the sight. But it was the metal of blades, a long bleeding sword and a short stabbing knife. They lay on a shirt with only one mend (a tear at the breast) and on breeks of good wool, and long legging boots with a fine jinking buckle and a hard steel cap.

'Clothes for your christening,' said Margaret Graham, 'if you'll ride to the Old Man and make him fit for the priest.'

Martin Farrell felt the weapons reach for his grasp. His fingers closed round the hilts. Most strange . . . Most familiar . . . He hefted their weight. His heart hammered like horsemen who rode the hot-trod, muscles roped in his wrists.

'Aye,' he said, dreamy, 'aye, I'll do as ye ask.'

Was ever a lover so eager to strip to the skin? Martin tore off his rags to put that shirt on, but the Galloway fiddler, never a man to be made blind by the moon, saw the ghosts of five Grahams rise from the kist – how, with fingers like marsh-gas, they helped Martin dress. Under his breath he whispered a curse.

'Now sleep by my fire, lad.' With lips pale as wild roses, the Widow leaned toward Martin and gave him one kiss. Then she motioned to Hughie, 'Come, escort me.'

43

The fiddler watched them away up the tower steps, watched our lad finger the fine stuff and thumbed each string of his fiddle. It twanged a discordance. He tapped his boot with his bow and, under his hat brim, his brow creased in a frown.

'Martin?' he said, but the lad did not turn. So with hands weeping and bloody he wrapped his fiddle in oiled skin, tugged the straps of his pack.

A cold bite of night wind tugged Martin's hair. The fiddler had opened the door before Martin Farrell turned in alarm.

'You'll no leave me!'

'To Hell wi' ye, Martin!' The fiddler's eyes burned. 'May your path there be a merry one and longer than mine! Ach! Like the rest of them, you're born blinded by blood! Can you not see the door, choose your own path? Ask yourself this when you're sober – who left who on this dark night? Ye fool!'

'Fiddler!' cried Martin.

But the tall stranger never looked back. His fiddle clattered on his shoulder as he strode to the gate. The Widow's strong wine seemed to tilt the whole world. Too late to cry, 'Friend!' Too late to cry, 'Wait!'

Surprised at his watch, the gateman cried, 'Ho!' but the fiddler was gone to the night before he'd run down to slam home the bolt.

At the door of her chamber, the Widow turned to the stoat.

'Hughie Lackland, I can see every secret you hid in your heart.' She smiled at her great-nephew as his face blenched. 'Would ye fulfil the high part of your destiny?'

'Aye, aye,' whispered Hughie. 'Aye, that I would!' His

lips flecked with spittle. Oh, there's many a proud fellow sorely misled, believing their fortune is what they would choose to have!

'Then,' says the Widow, 'let the youth live. When your time comes to act, you'll know the sign sure enough.'

Hughie nodded and smiled – a smile like the oil poured on poison when it's corked in the glass. He bade her goodnight. Aye, he was thinking, he could wait for the lad, but the tune of that bold insolent beggar, the Galloway fiddler, had twisted his guts. And of him had she spoken? He was sure she had not.

ammastide, Lammastide ... And who'd risk a wedding but a barley corn king? Oh, Will Armstrong what have ye done? Bring the confessor. Fill up my cup! It's a sweet tune on the chanter-pipe to think of that lass. Here's an health to Anne Eliot, to her in-breath, her out-breath and to all that her sighs make rise and fall! Ach, we're long enough dead! Let the flesh pay its dues!

Aye, but let's not be forgetting that each season turns. Elder and briar rose fade in the sun, harebell and yarrow likewise in their turn. In the blackmailed land the Armstrongs held thrall, the barley grew golden in each small man's strip. Up on the moorsides with their summering cows, they frowned and looked down at the soft sway of the wind which rippled each shining beard. Hushed like men guilty or planning a raid, they sat by a thornbush to sharpen a scythe, whispered to neighbours, watched for smoke in the sky.

Still, it held quiet in the Borders. The day after the wedding, the Armstrongs, Nixons, Neils, Eliots and Kerrs ran a horse-betting race on the green river plain. Hearing this planned, poor men bolted their doors. They expected a bickering, a letting of blood. But, no! Nebless Nick, a little light nowt won the race, silver spurs, and the great men of each family drank to his health. Very strange ... Shaking his head, fingering his scythe, each small man unbolted his door and crept out.

A warm wind went on blowing up from the South. Bolder, they strayed to a field's edge, thumbed off a husk and tested the nearness of harvest in the flour of the hard grain they nipped with their teeth.

Strange tales ran. A black cow had born a two-headed white calf. A drover had passed from Dumfries to Penrith

46

with not one horn of his herd going amiss – though he'd passed through a snowstorm on Bewcastle waste. The Archbishop of Glasgow had cursed all reiving men.

But, strange among tales, two little ones ran – that the Old Man was looking for a peat-cutter's son. The other? That in the evergreen dark of the dead Graham hall, where nothing had stirred for fourteen long years save the Widow's black hem, music was heard.

Summer sun talk, words swapped like flagons of water between reapers and gleaners. Young mothers and old men are left to guard cattle as families creep down at dusk to the fields. *Harvest*.

Men move together in the flour-scented night. Quiet cattle watch them scythe under a moon that grows huge, rises yellow, trembles above. A boy in a tree watches for horsemen or for fire in the sky.

Ah, scythe, stook and whetstone, the last squeal of rabbits imprisoned in stalks. A child toddles to its mother clutching a mouse.

Hold your breath. Can it be true? Can it be that threshing will fill lop-lugged sacks with good grain?

Stories are whispered as the reapers creep home. When Will Armstrong forded the river after the horse race, a salmon leapt clean over his saddle. 'Jock's Alan,' it said.

Anne Eliot? They say the bride's cheek has turned pale, that she's taken to saying long prayers to keep from his bed.

But what of the fiddler? So then, ye asked . . . Kick the log on the fire to a shower of sparks. Aye, let's raise a cup, here's a hale toast to us, to all our true friends, though few they might be, aye, and most o' them dead . . .

What of it? We knew them. Can't that be enough? I'll wipe my face on my sleeve. Death pecks at our ribs between each heartbeat, each breath, and still the sun rises though he feathers his nest.

Say a prayer for the fiddler. Aye, if you will. It's no burden to him. He died in that red dawn more alive than most live.

So, away! Away with all mourning! In this debatable time it trails like the stink of smoke blackening cornfields. It's the snuff of inheritors, a tithe to the priest. I've seen many a good woman's face wrinkled to ruin by sniff after sniff. Let's drink to his spirit, his music, his life! His corpse, it's to lie on the moss until his white ribs are a harp for the wind.

So then, ye asked . . . Fill up my cup! If I salt my liquor at all it's with tears for the stoat. Aye, Hughie Graham. The foul, twisty brute. For him we should weep good and long. And why? In the whole of his life he never once kissed as a lover nor whistled a note.

But what of the fiddle, her swan neck of pear wood greased dark over years by the fine fiddler's hand? And the good horse-hair bow? If you'll give over greeting and listen, I'll tell.

That dawn a man on a grey mare rode down from the Rigg. We've met him before. On the night that sot-drunken nothing, I mean the man Farrell, cried tongueless glabber as he was thrown to the boar. Aye, it's Neb Corbie, the industrious crow, surveying the land to see what pickings the night may have left.

He'd slept close by the river, been woken by the splash of hooves in the water, the soft snort of the grey mare as she smelled her own kind. With his thumb in her nostrils, he'd stayed hidden in whins and watched Hughie Graham kneel in the shallows, with fistfuls of gravel, scrubbing his hands.

He'd heard what he'd said to the wolfheads who rode with him. 'Let the auld bitch play her game wi' the lad. She foretells that he'll see the death of Old Man Armstrong! Auld spider, let her web catch its flies! And when it does? I'm ready and you'll be the chief of all Hughie Graham's guests!'

Oh, Neb Corbie, a big quiet man with a dangerous trade, whose heart always beat steady (he'd a complexion under his whiskers most women would envy), he'd seen the dark stains floating downstream. When the riders had gone, he mounted his mare and trailed their track back where it led through the sweet dew to the deed they had done.

So he rode from the hill and the man he found slain – aye, the Galloway fiddler – he'd known as a friend. Travellers both, plying their trades, they had shared a night fire and a cup and watched the stars fade into dawn, aye, more than once.

With a creak of worn leather, Corbie climbed from the saddle. He stood, tall and still, until the sun climbed behind him and the corpse of the fiddler stretched like his own shadow as the light revealed the malice of wounds. Neb Corbie, with no allegiance to houses, no fear of death, found for once in his life, his heart beating fast.

At last he reached for the fiddle where it had fallen in mud, rescued the bow from where it had been flung in the long grass under a thorn. A lark and her young flew up in his face but he blew them away with a great gusting breath, crying, 'This fiddle has work as the sky needs your song! Away! Away! Wee brothers and sisters! Leave this undertaking to the black feathered ones – crows sweeten the air in debatable times!'

Then he looked at the corpse of our Galloway man. 'You'll no suffer the joint aches though ye sleep on damp ground. Sleep well, dear friend. What I take I won't sell. I ken you knew the road that you took. Fate's been your friend, for, to be sure, the slow road of starvation would have been yours come the Winter by the cruel state of your hands.'

He picked up the fiddler's hat, then mounted the mare and with one last look back, said, 'I'll find your apprentice. I'll see your fiddle played well.'

Ah, but dawn's swiftly passed and in the wide, peaceable Borders the black cattle graze. The dew's sweet. The wind shifts to the west. The wife of a poor man tests its strength with a spit on her finger, fetches her flail and, with her lads keeping watch, helps her good man winnow grain from the chaff. Crows lift, bow on the breeze, as the ravens pay their respects to what the night's left.

And what of our lad? Martin Farrell woke in a new shirt, boots of stitched leather, a sword by his hand and the 'clickit-clack-clack' of the Widow's swift shuttle as it flies through the loom.

He lifts his head from the plank and sees her in sunlight at the doorway weaving white cloth. On the board, white steam rises from porridge. There's milk in a jug. And a spoon, can ye believe it? A spoon! To break his long fast.

This boy, what shall we call him? He woke and sat upright and thought himself blessed. Here was a new life, not like the old one, where if his head's drumming it's not from a blow but from drinking sweet wine! You call him weakling, judge his name Fool?

Judgement comes easy. As a fool that knows himself well, my heart hurts for our fool . . . He watches the Widow as she sits at her work. Why did he fear her? Her hair's tucked in a snood and if her bones crack and click in tune to her weaving? Why, it's the stiff clatter of the joints of the old . . .

What's Heaven? Do you need me to tell? Ask the fiddler if you're wanting a tune. Here's what I know. For most it's the place that we long for when we long for a home. And there's many a false knight disguised as a preacher would show us the road.

So then, name the lad Fool? Whisht! Martin's young. He lost his mother before his babble had words. The man he called father is in a peat-sodden grave . . . He wakes to the day in a house built of stone! Oats to break fast! And if the fiddler's gone, what of it? To be sure, he was nothing more than a friend of two days. Why, he's walking the moss and crossing the moors. Ghosts reach from the kist, cloak Martin's eyes . . .

Many a young man watches an elder woman as she bends to her work and thinks that Jerusalem will be found in her hands. He wants milk and honey – the nectar of babes still cauled from the womb. But *want's* a strong potion, a poison, a gnaw at the belly no porridge can cure. Ask Hughie Graham! Aye, that kind of hunger can murder a neighbour, make Heaven a trough . . .

Watch Martin Farrell. As he walked down the hall the soft leather of good boots kissed both his knees and the point of the scabbard tupped the flagstones. The very song of his new clothes seemed to make him a man. The shankle of spurs! Did he pity the crookety servant crouched in the hearth rattling irons among wood ash? No! Away to Hell. No! It gave power to his stride to see some other creature's head bent to the dirt. Ware, Martin Farrell! That's the way of the stoat.

'Lady,' said Martin, 'will you lend me a mount to ride to my fate?'

Margaret Graham? Did she smile? No, she silenced the

loom. She was cunning with grief, had a winter of patience. And the boy stood before her – she could see at a glance that like some spirited colt he would charge at a thorn bush yet shy at a leaf. 'Hush, bide, be still, lad. For all that I spoke, I'd not have ye go. Would I lose my lost daughter's son? With my man and my own sons all dead in the earth?'

Martin thought of the hovel in which he'd been raised. 'Lady,' he said, 'what brought the house of the Grahams so low?'

'The knives of the Armstrongs, of your murderous kin.'

'Armstrongs? My kin!' Martin Farrell cried.

Aye, Margaret Graham thought as she watched him sink to his haunches, what brings strength to the steel? The hammering blows. When you're shod in your fate, it's then I'll let you ride. I'll temper your will.

'Wounds o' God . . .' whispered Martin, his head in his hands. 'Tell me who I am . . . Lady, tell me my name . . .'

The fiddler's ghost rose on one elbow and cried from the moss, 'Be glad that ye have none!'

But the lad's hunched by the Widow, deaf to the advice of the curlew, the sweet prayer of the lark.

'Hooo . . .' whispered Margaret Graham. 'Listen well . . .' The summer breeze billowed the winding sheet that hung from her loom. It fell quiet as snow as she told of a moonless night in midwinter, near sixteen years passed . . . The reivers are riding. Iron frost grips the earth, ice shatters and drums beneath galloping hooves. And the house of the Grahams wakes to the wild cries of the Armstrongs driving off their black cattle. The blood of their herdsman spots the white snow like red berries. Crimson flames roar at the gate. It's been drenched with pitch and set on fire with a brand.

'Woe to the Old Man to have ridden that raid! And a curse on the Armstrongs! Greater thieves never lived!'

The Grahams rose to the fray and rode in pursuit, but by a devious road. When the Armstrongs thought themselves safe, what did they find? The Grahams before them with twenty roused neighbours to add to their strength. A black line of riders as black as the night and all in steel bonnets. The Armstrongs stampeded the cattle and tried to make good their escape up the steep valley side. But here's the luck of the Grahams! Rynion Armstrong, eldest son of the Old Man, was thrown from his horse.

The jubilant Grahams taught him to dance.

'They hanged him?' says Martin.

'Aye, by his own belt.'

A deed of revenge, the law of the Borders, the misrule of men. It rolls like a boulder pushed down a hill. For there is the Old Man with his furious eye, humiliation his bread. The death of an heir. That night's work struck him hard and strengthened the hand of the Grahams, his foe.

Aye, he swore deep revenge and bided his time.

For a year, the land seemed to lie quiet. Ah, peaceable time. There were deaths among Eliots and over by Jedburgh the Kerrs grew fat on the ransom of prisoners they kept in their pit. So it went to the Martinmas when the Armstrongs had news. Margaret Graham's young daughter, Bess Graham, had been seen dressed in fine furs and ribbons. She rode with her brothers to be guests at a feast over the hill.

Did the Galloway fiddler play for the dancing that night? Of that I've no knowledge and so I can't tell. But woe to the Grahams as they laughed there and supped. Outside, in the forest the ambush was set. The Old Man with his second son, Gibb, (aye, the one that died from the bite of a dog) and forty hard men stood in the shadows under the trees.

In her chamber, in the tower, Margaret Graham combed her long hair but dropped the comb with a cry when she looked in the mirror and no reflection came there.

Cold was the news that came with the dawn. Four sons dead and Bess Graham carried off slung over the Old Man's saddle.

What he stole from her no man could return.

Can Martin Farrell say *father*? The word cracked in his throat. Though he kneels in bright sunlight it seems that his soul is falling forever into the dark.

And, 'Hush,' says the Widow. 'May he turn forever in Hell on a spit! He imprisoned your mother – my bonny wee daughter till the night of your birth. Though my husband made both raid and petition to set the lass free.'

What didn't she say? That her man had turned yellow with chagrin at this ruin of his honour, that the ill luck of the Grahams made neighbours turn away. Oh, the star of the Old Man was rising that year in a sky ruled by Mars.

And they say that Bess Graham gave birth in a blizzard. Where? In a byre. Among the dung of the cattle and the stale steaming straw. And what were the shadows she saw on the wall in the light of the tallow? Women bending their heads and reaching soft hands to the child?

No. It seemed then to Martin that he knew this from dreams. He covered his ears with his hands. Crushed his eyes closed. Saw the shadows of helmets and pikes as the Old Man kicked open the door and in swirled the snow.

'*Marry the first outlander we bring ye or else bury the whelp now . . .*'

Poor prisoner. Poor lady, with a babe she'd sworn not to

touch if she lived through the birth, felt his mouth plug her nipple, bowed her head to the choice and a strand of her hair was clutched by the babe's fist. She found that her hands pressed him close to her breast.

The Armstrongs brought her a thief – the wee man they called Farrell. He'd been cut down from the hanging tree and still wore the hemp collar. His wedding gear? Aye. The frayed noose.

The lass was a beauty! The child wasn't his. What of it? Here was a fate that seemed sweeter than the rope's dance.

Aye, the Old Man's revenge on the house of the Grahams . . . Fourteen years on, watch the Widow's hand shake. She pushes the shuttle through the threads on the loom but finds that it sticks.

'A pocket thief, a chancer, was wed to my daughter. Now Martin *Farrell*, does your name seem enough?

'The news killed my man. He ailed from that day.'

What didn't she say? How he'd cursed his own daughter with words wild as whips, crying how she'd have done well to crack the ice on the river and flung herself in, aye! And the whelp! Better that than to live in such shame! Bring down his good name! How, raid after raid, he'd rode on these Armstrongs seeking honour in death. But who was the Old Man to grace him with that?

How complete in the art of revenge was the Old Man, to harry this Graham, murder his allies, but never once touch a hair of his head. Till, babbling spittle, the man died from a stroke, abandoned by friends who found him ill-starred and none but his Widow to weep on his grave.

'That very same night, as I was threading a needle to sew him a shroud, and the hills gloated with beacons spreading the news, your mother, my daughter, took sudden and died . . .'

The tale of the Widow. Aye, in the Wakes week of Lammas, it moves like a cloud shadow over the bright barley fields.

On that same sunlit morning Anne Eliot woke to the cool scents of summer, the high song of the lark. She glanced at her husband. It was early. Will Armstrong slept. The sight made her press her hand to her breast bone as if she could pluck the pain from her heart. He lay, bonny, bold, a fine manly sight.

'Ah, husband,' she whispered. 'What will I give birth to? Must it for aye be a sword and a grave if our baby's a son? A black shawl for a daughter?'

With a sad hand she reached out to touch the soft silk of his hair, the spun wire of his beard. She longed for a day when the peace of his face did not pass with the dawn. The longing of women in debatable times . . .

But that stillness was broken by a hoarse wild shout and a boot at the door. The cry of, 'Will! Rouse up man! Will! Will! Get up!'

And in stormed the Old Man, her father-in-law. He dragged back the cover, lifted the jack-coat from where it lay on the kist and dumped it down on Will Armstrong's bare ribs. Then he turned and stamped away down the stair with his son hurrying after, blinking sleep from his eyes, shrugging his arms into the coat's sleeves.

To Anne Eliot it seemed that the chamber rang like a tin bucket hit by a stick till sunlight and stillness reclaimed the shocked air. She went to her mirror and found in her own frowning reflection it was true what she saw. Could it be that she'd seen the whites of *both* the Old Man's stone eyes and on him smelled *fear*?

She shrugged her shawl round her and quietly followed after, her bare toes seeking the tread of the cool, worn, spiral stair until she neared the well bottom. And that's where she waited, hidden and silent, for what she might hear.

'Will,' hissed the Old Man, 'do ye dream?' Did he wait for an answer? No, he paced to the hearth, clenched his fists together until the joints cracked. 'I never!' he hissed at the cold ash. Then he turned on his heel and his eye had the red glare. 'I never! Not once in my life!' Rare agitation! 'Other men dream! Armstrongs watch, wake and act!'

And what of Will Armstrong? Why, he's little more than a great golden brute. Will? He has no more will than dry barley straw. That thin burnish on him is the shine of a spear that can't choose its target without a hand or an eye. And the eye and the hand for all of his days had been the Old Man's.

But, whisht, strange to tell, as he harkened to his father on this sunlit morning a deep tremor seemed to start in his shoulder, just like the ripples that judder when a fly settles on the flank of a bull.

The Old Man sat at the board, squinted down at his thumbs and clicked the nails together. 'But last night I dreamed . . .' he said softly. 'And woke in so wet a lather I thought my bed filled with blood. Will, I dreamed I was hunted by a black hare and harried to death . . .'

'Away!' cries Will. 'Who could put the eye on *ye*? Ye'd the touch of a fever on a hot Lammas night!'

'No, Will. What I had was a warning and a warning's a weed that grows in the soil of doubt. I should have rid myself of that whelp and its mother before it was spawned.'

'What whelp?'

'The one I bought with the spare coins I flung at Bess Graham and then kept alive for the pleasure of watching her father writhe like an eel on the hook.'

He clapped his hands on the board, stood and smiled a bit smile.

'Come! It's fine weather for hunting. You and I can make sport of the game Jock's Alan put up.'

Aye, to be fair, let's give Will Armstrong his due. The tremor turned to a shudder that caught at his voice. 'The lad you had watched by the peat-cutter up on the moss? He's half an Armstrong. Half our own blood . . .'

'Aye, well. So be it. When we've tracked him down we can cut him in two and leave one half for the crows and, if ye still desire it, bring back our half.'

Anne Eliot? Ach, do you need telling? She stumbled back up the stairs and now both her hands were pressed to her mouth.

Do ye shift? Give the bit cough? Are ye sullen my tale's no of great deeds? Raids endeavoured? Fearsome fights between men? Is your belly not full? Fetch a new tallow, this one's puddled down. Let's light the new from the old one; now bring me more wine. Here, hah! See, steady, steady! Fill my cup to the brim! Aye. Gentle – ah man, like a hand on a breast, fill, aye! Hah! See ye! Stay your hand! See ye! How the wine stands above my filled cup, over the brim!

Add one more drop, Mother of Love! Add one tear! Whoah! And it floods! Ah! It sets me to thinking of Anne Eliot's eyes when the tears stood . . .

So then, pass me my fiddle. I'll play for ye. There's bread on the board.

Here's my hat. Here. Pass it around. I'll not say a word till it's lined with your coins.

Aye. Pass it back.

A curse on your charity! I can still see the crown! But the fire roars at the lumb, the hearth glimmers like Hell! Watch. One after one I'll toss these coins in!

You don't care for the jest? Aye, by the skrem of your face

I can tell. Ye poor dogs. Then I'll keep your coins, if you'll fill your cup with gold dust from Sunday to Sunday. When you're dying of thirst, we'll speak again.

Away! Away! I'll tell the tale's end . . .

Our lad, Martin Farrell – aye, let's still give him that name, though he rode from the bleak tower in the clouts of a Graham. What was he? Where was he? Is he shod in his fate? As he rode through the forest on a bone⁄spavined mount (aye, the last horse in Margaret Graham's stable), cobwebs clagged his face and twigs lashed his eyes. He thought of the tales the dead peat⁄cutter told on those nights he had liquor in a fat⁄handled jug. Of the freaks he had seen, or so the man said, in the Michaelmas fair – the man who had breasts, the lass with a beard, the two⁄headed lamb, a dwarf led by a string, the bull with a pizzle so long it was kept strapped to its nose⁄ring.

I should be among them, so the lad thought, to be sired by an Armstrong and born by a Graham. What ever else is there? But to carve in the flesh of my kinsfolk my own bloody name . . .

Had he forgotten the fiddler? I'd say so, in his shock and his blame.

What had he? A horse and a saddle that had seen better days, the crookety servant to act as a guide back to the high road. He hears the crabbed creature's chuggering breath as they climb from the trees to where the last branches part on the ridge. And there is the light! The huge sky of the Borders on a sweet Lammas day, the sweep of two kingdoms all to be seen from the long vacant edge!

They break from the forest to the lapwing's quizzling

'qweep', the bubbling curlew like the throat of a live spring in the sodden peat.

The crookety servant, a dog long kept in a shed, shivers with palsy and blinks raw rheumy eyes.

Martin slid from the saddle (truth to tell it was with some relief – he'd known little of horses and walked most of his life on his two feet) and stood by his mount. Above him the buzzard sailed in slow circles on the spiralling air and, unknown to Martin, a crow watched from a distance among a copse of old thorns.

'God's Teeth!' cried the crookety fellow, holding his knee caps and squinting around. 'It's a kingdom! All I see wi' my good eye could one day be yours! From that far beacon hill all the way to the ford! The lands o' the Armstrongs and Grahams grabbed by your hand . . .'

But our lad stood quite silent and looked at the land. He listened to blether – the crookety servant away from the Widow had strong opinions on murder, how best to achieve it. For the Old Man, his father? Be a child, run into his arms with a sob, then ram the hug of a short stabbing blade up between his third ribs. Then ride like the wind to Will Armstrong – ach, this must be on the day they're rounding the yearlings – to tell of his death. Take a pin and strong poison, scratch his thigh as he mounts up, let death do the rest.

Martin Farrell? He stares at his shadow. He finds his jaw aches.

The wee shrivelled servant snigged up his lip's edge and a laugh whistled out between his last seven teeth. 'And Anne Eliot. They say that her nipples are red as the berries against her white skin – take my advice . . .'

But the short blade jumps sudden into Martin Farrell's

hand and skids on the old crither's turkey neck skin. He screams like a hare in the jaws of a fox! Martin Farrell has his scalp hair in his young hands and the blade on his throat. A great fire rose in him – the wild fire of the soul that can blacken or cleanse a young heart. He heard the fiddler's wild music and let the man drop. The crookety servant fell like a sack, shrieking he's murthered! He howls for last rites! Why? Away! There's nothing more than a scrape on his craw bristles – a scratch like a thread and on it are strung twelve beads of blood.

What of our lad? The agony's his. He watches the old spider scrabble away. He watches the blade twitch in his hand, divining for blood and he gave a great sigh and let the knife drop. 'If I make him the first then he'll not be the last . . .

There he stood in the wind. For how long? What's time to the heart? Some say a year and a day, some say forty nights. His horse ate white flowers and blew the seed clocks of thistles over the sour moorland grass. Clouds badged the valleys with sudden banners of light. He stood till the sky had gone blue as the heather, then the dust-pink of the dog rose, as royal purple and shredded with gold as the robe of the faerie who wooed young Tamlin. Dusk creeps from the hollows. The horse wets his muzzle hairs to black in the sweet drizzle of dew. The wind falls like a feather, stills on the boy's lips as if all breath had gone.

At last the old horse snuffed Martin's back, called his soul home. 'Away . . .' whispered Martin. He found strength in his fingers to unsaddle and unbridle the beast.

'Away, now, brother. Go free . . .'

He shouldered his sword like a traveller's stick and as the dusk deepened trudged up to the ridge. And what was he thinking? Of the fiddler's last words. Aye, and with longing and most bitterly.

Who saw him, the lad, at that twilit hour? The moon rising? He passed the thorn copse and saw nothing more than a shadow beside a grey boulder beneath the bent trees. But there the Crow watched. The black tattered mawkin that proud men mock yet secretly dread for his skill at divining the price to be paid for all hidden deeds. He took a deep breath of the air Martin left in his wake, a snuff of his soul, then blew his nose on his sleeve.

He led the mare from the thicket, swung up his bulk and with a quiet click of his tongue and a press of his knees, he rode after our lad where he walked, silhouetted, on the high starlit ridge. And the fiddler's hat was perched on the saddle's high pommel, while the bow and the fiddle hung from a strap and sang a low tune against the mare's flank.

Martin walked with his head bowed. He shifted the sword from shoulder to shoulder. Its weight was a load. Once, he fell to his knees to lick dew from the grasses, his thirst seemed to blaze.

And Neb Corbie reined in his mare while he watched him. Oh, the Crow, do you need me tell ye? He was one of the wise.

When Martin rose and trudged on, he gave him good distance, then when he judged ready, he followed behind. The wind dropped. The moon, waning, gave the great constellations a place in the skies. On the turf of the moors the hooves of the grey mare made scarcely a noise.

Have pity on them, on all lonely travellers as they stumble in darkness in search of a road.

Martin went on. Moths rose round his boots to dance to the moon. Mother of Love! Was he weary? And now a deep hunger gnawed at his belly. He fell to his knees by the dry bed of a stream and put a pebble under his tongue to suck on, just as he had done as a child when the peat-cutter stacked sods and he played alone. That's when he heard the slow drum of hooves and turned in alarm. And there was the black stranger who'd dragged him from the hovel into that fateful dawn. Did he fear him? Aye, he found that he did, more than a little, and that fear stilled his tongue.

With a swish of his stinking black tatters, the Crow climbed from the saddle. The starlight flashed a glint in his eyes as he came towards Martin, patting his rags until he found what he sought. A wee tinder box. 'So, I've the flint, there's dry heather to burn. Will ye share the night's fire and whatever ye own? I've a flask and a loaf.'

Martin Farrell? Oh, at that invitation, his head bowed in shame.

'Neb Corbie,' he said.

'Hah! Aye, that's one o' my names!'

Martin sighed deeply. He lifted the sword and held it toward Corbie in his two outstretched hands. 'I have ye to thank for saving my life, so it seems, but I've nothing to give ye unless you'll take this . . .'

'Lad!' the Crow roared in swift anger. 'My nose liked ye was all! And would you make life a transaction, a debting, a count on the fingers of who ye owe or have paid? That's the way of the foul miser doomed to losing his hoard!' The Crow spat on the ground. 'Besides, that sword stinks to high Heaven. No, lad wi' no name, ye can't shrug off that load . . .'

The blood rose in Martin and scalded his cheeks for the Crow had a hard beak, quick to seek out a wound. He tried to deny the hurt that he felt, crying, 'Hah! Stranger, I could throw this sword down, let it rust on the moors!'

64

Neb Corbie shrugged and quietly set to, pulling the heather for a fire and a bed. He soon had a blaze and a fine springy mattress on which he spread his dank rug. He took his flask and his loaf from the saddle bag, broke open the bread and fed half to his horse, then with a grunt set his bulk by his hearth and again broke in two pieces the last of the loaf. 'Here,' he held out a wedge. 'You can no more cast that blade from you than I can eat stones.'

In the dance of the flames he saw Martin's set face, the thrust of his chin. That made the Crow laugh. Laying the food on the ground, he put the flask to his mouth and pulled out the wood stopper with his strong white teeth. He took a deep swig then, 'Yah!' He screwed shut his eyes and spat on the ground. 'Nails o' God! The look on your face is souring my wine! If you'll no sit then away wi ye! Let your proud Graham league boots march ye to Hell! It seems I was wrong. I saw ye back there on the ridge when you chose not to spill the thin blood of the Widow's poor dog. Hah! I thought a light danced in ye then! Now I see that you're blind, proud and stubborn. See ye there! See you standin'! Lost in the dark and yet will ye rest by the fire, crack your stiff knees to set and share bread!' He huffed a long breath. 'Ach, lad, what binds you to that terrible blade!'

Our lad, in his need, his heart longed to trust him, yearned to confide, but it was his turn to spit and cry out in rage, 'And if I tell ye, Neb Corbie, for all your fine words upon debting, who will ye sell this secret to? What price do *I* fetch in your trade? Why did you save me? I'd be better off slain!' Martin hefted the sword high with the strength of two hands and stepped toward Corbie, and the ghost light that ran through the clothes from the kist gave a murderous fury and power to his arms. 'It's you I should run clean through to the bone, stinking villain! But three nights passed, I knew my name! Martin Farrell! Farrell! Why didn't ye leave me to fight for the one man who raised me? I coulda died wi' him . . .'

Do you need me tell? On Martin's young face the tears coursed down. 'What cruel sport have ye wi' me? Black, filthy carrion! It's you I've to blame!' The blade sheered through the night and sliced under the stars towards the Crow's head.

Did it kill him? Let me wax mathematical. The force of the swing took Martin full circle. (Away, our peat-cutter's stepson was never a swordsman.) The first quadrant was rage; the second blind terror at what he was doing as he saw the compassionate calm in the Crow's fire-lit eyes. The third quadrant? A drop into Hell, dread and remorse for what he had done. And there, in the fourth, he sank to his knees and the blade clattered from him into the fire. A red shower of sparks crashed into the air and some fell upon him, singeing his shirt and burning his hair.

Neb Corbie? He'd bobbed low his head.

Now he sat up.

Wull O' The Shroud, a rare gifted man. He waited in peace, with a slow beating heart, for the lad's breath to steady, for the boy to open his eyes. The grey mare staled, a sweet odorous piss. The dry wind lifted the scent of the barley from down in the valley where a poor man worked quietly with his sickle toward the last sheaf.

At last Martin felt a strong arm round his shoulder urging him up, and clear crystal spring water poured from the flask on to his lips. And there's a scent in his nostrils, the perfume of roses. It came from the tatters of Neb Corbie's sleeve as, with a firm hand under his oxter, he urged Martin to stand, brought him to the fire and bade him sit down.

The lad stared at him in wonder. Why? Because he's not stretched on the ground? Aye, and then, nay. No, this wonder grew greater, deeper, and wider, as the Crow swiped at him with his outstretched hand. Did he deliver a blow? Again, no. He brushed a spark from Martin's shoulder where a cinder had set to a smoulder the old Graham cloth. In all his short life, to have raised his own voice had seen Martin Farrell struck to the ground with a fist or pelted with peat sods. Or, if Farrell had coppers, to be left for three days as the man rode with the drovers to some far away inn.

Dark patterns of blue, grey and dull red made serpents on the long blade of the sword as it lay in the fire. The Crow saw where the boy's gaze settled, and with his large, grimy hand, reached for the hilt and raised up the weapon from the smoke and the blaze.

'Tcha!' he gobbed on the steel. His spittle made a sizzling small ball. It fizzled. Was gone. He set down the sword on the moor grass between them. Each dry plant by its edge shrivelled and smouldered then burst into flame. Aye, on the ground, it scorched, flared, and blackened the shape of itself.

Then it cooled. Martin said, 'I tried to kill ye . . .'

Neb Corbie shrugged. 'Aye. I knew that you would, son of Bess Graham . . .' And now here's a marvel! 'I'm glad that you did.'

Martin Farrell? What's this in his lugs?

The Crow nodded, bit at the loaf. 'Aye, now I can sleep safe on my bed.' He gave over chewing and looked hard at the lad. 'If true murder was in you, ye'd have stayed your hand till I slept. As for my trade with you? I seek out what's hidden, aye, and return it. And there's rarely a man nor a woman want their own stinking carrion brought to the light. Some think they can bury it wi' handfuls of gold, but some weep, sigh and grow strong, aye, for each one that does the weft and warp alters in the weave of the world . . . So then, Martin Farrell, now ye ken what it is to wield that weapon in rage, will ye no find a smith? It's a strong length o' steel to make a fine sickle blade!'

With woe in his heart, our lad shook his head. 'I fear that I cannot. I gave the Widow my word . . .'

Says the Crow slowly, 'To kill Old Man Armstrong or to be killed?'

Martin nodded. He could scarce meet the man's eyes. Corbie rose with a roar that startled the mare and set her to dancing, then he strode a great circle in the border of darkness between the night and the light from the flames. With his black rags flailing, his long hooked neb, he seemed to shift shape to the shadow of ravens that flock to the field when the battle is done. The kinsmen lie slain. 'You were tricked by your own honest longing for kin!' he cawed from the dark as he swooped and tore up a bush of the strong-rooted whin. It flew from his hand to smash into the fire and burst into flame. 'Oh spare me temptation! To curse Margaret Graham . . . No! I'll no do it! That lady's known woes enough to sour any soul! Hapless Widow! What have ye done? Where's the hantle of men that should ha' roused to your aid in these foul times?'

Now he stood in the circle stamped by the Crow, strength rose in Martin, strength of his own. 'I'm not afraid to go to my father and die at his hand if that is my road!'

Out of the night, the ravens swooped down. He found himself grasped by the stern, tender talons of Neb Corbie's hands. 'No! There's a way! You have courage? Aye. Then tear off this finery, strip off that false shirt, those boots and the hose and throw them in the fire. Set them to burn!'

'Would you have me stand naked as the day I was born?'

'Aye,' the Crow shook him. 'And quickly! There's still time before midnight. You're sore tested to trust me but it's all I can do for ye. Will you heed my words?'

Martin Farrell finds his blood beating loudly. And what was he thinking? Of the fiddler as they sat at the board. Of the fiddler with his long palms all bloody. Ah, then was the time he should have paid heed! *Trust only one man.* As he stood in the Crow's urgent grip, he found that he did and that man was himself. 'Aye,' he said. 'Aye, I'll do what you tell me.'

'Then all this long night you must sit here naked and never stray once from the circle of light, *no matter who calls ye*, but should any shade, no matter how terrible, rise from the dark, *invite them to come to ye, and do what they ask.*'

Did Martin Farrell tremble? I would say so. Wouldn't ye? Neb Corbie let him go. 'You must stay until dawn. There's no more aid I can give ye. If you still have your wits at sun up we'll meet again.'

And with that, the Crow left him, swung up on his mare and galloped away across the night moor. Some say Martin heard the drum of hooves overhead and saw the beating of wings against the bright stars. That's as may be. Whisht! With hands that shook with more than fear's palsy, Martin tore at his clothes. Some task! The cloth and the leather seemed to cleave to him. If you'd seen how he wrestled out of that shirt you'd have thought you were watching a loon, aye, a crazy, tearing his skin. He was sobbing for breath as he lay bare on the ground to fight with his boots. And with a wild cry he set them to cinder in the whin's golden flame. All night that bush burned steady and was never consumed, and our lad knelt by it,

69

naked and trembling at that fire by the dry bed of the stream.

Is it true, what I tell you? Fill up my cup. No truer tale has ever come from my tongue.

Can you hear it? There! And again! The crow of the cockerel in the hour before dawn. The night's at its darkest. Aye, it's the time when the dying man turns his face to the wall, when the good wife attending the childbed hears the infant's first mewl. Will you watch through it with me? The tale's soon done, then I'll bid you good morrow, shoulder my pack and be on my way when the smoke wisps from snuffed tallows at the rise of the sun.

On this, the third night on from the wedding, see Margaret Graham. She sits long at her weaving with the poor crookety servant crouched at her heel, the old dog. Once, she reaches her hand to stroke his grey head, to steady the rattle which threatens his wind/pipe and murmurs, 'Stay a while longer. You were ever faithful . . . Stay a while yet.'

At that affection the crither opened raw eyes, watched as she took her small shears from her girdle where they hung by the keys, as she snipped the tail from each knotted thread.

Hughie Graham? Did he play strutting master, sat at the board plotting a murder? Or sleeping one off in his bed? Did he play at the dice with his wolfheads? No. I've heard tell he was out in the dark of the courtyard, hoping no one would see him, as he hauled on the worm/eaten winch at the well. Into each slopping bucket he plunged his hands. The blood of the Galloway fiddler oiled the water with a swirling stain. But for all his wiping of fingers it wouldn't be gone.

The Widow, at last, took to cutting the length of the cloth from the loom.

'Lady,' the crookety servant heaved air in his lungs, 'I loved ye.'

'I know that you did. And you'll sleep at my feet now my work is done.'

And, with the cloth over her arm, she stooped, kissed his

71

forehead, and bade him take word to Hugh Lackland to come to her room. 'When he leaves, return to my chamber, for we must lie down.'

So then. They say the stoat was brought to her where she stood swathed in her winding sheet, her glowing shawl. Where she stood by the mirror with her back to him as she combed out her hair. Hughie Graham? Why, he watched in wonder as the need of all flesh fell away and her face in the glass grew more and more fair.

Aye, the stoat, with damp sleeves, wrung his hands at his back and watched, with what wrenching? There was the Widow, wrapped in white cloth, as for a wedding, and her eyes looked on him from the glass of the mirror. He glimpsed all the sweetness in life he had missed.

Did that set him to pondering? No! He clenched a smile on his teeth.

'Hughie Lackland, what more sign do ye seek? Would ye reap the reward for how you have served me?'

'Oh, Lady, I would!'

'Then it is done. The last child on earth with a claim on my blood sleeps by a ford beyond the high Rigg. Seek him at dawn if ye'd get what ye own, but dismiss your wolfheads. Seek him yourself. Take no company.'

The stoat? He found the maggot he'd nourished for all of his years seemed to have come to the season to hatch! He found her words wise. He was thinking, it's true, there's not one of the bastards I trust. Take them wi' me, and they could turn upon me when I've sliced the lad's throat! 'On the Rigg? By the ford? Great-aunt, I'll go to it. I give you my word. Sleep in peace!'

The Widow, she watched as he bowed and scraped from her room, and murmured, 'I will.'

They say her poor crither, her grey hound, came and curled at her heels, and there the ache fled forever from his crookety bones.

And what of the Armstrongs? That self same day Will and the Old Man rode from the hall. They turned the steeds to the upland and, under a sky whistling with skylarks, made for the hovel which had been Farrell's home.

As they passed each poor strip of tenanted field, whole families stopped their work of the harvest and fell to their knees. Will saw how a thin mother, with force of sheer terror, pushed the heads of her toddlers down to a bow. The Old Man, he stared straight ahead and seemed not to see them, yet if one man had not done so, to be sure, he'd have tasted his whip.

Was Will Armstrong merry to be away hunting on this bright, peaceable day? Oh, if he'd had his spear, his hounds, and a clutch of companions there at his side, aye, to have flushed the quarry he would have been glad. The fire for the ride, the hunt, the battle all burned in his ruddy heart. But even his horse seemed to catch at his mood, and twice the beast stumbled as they went up the slope.

And once he looked back down at the tower and saw how his young wife had strayed through the gate, how she stood among the flowers of the field with her hand pressed to her breast bone as if the place hurt. Though he knew that she watched him, he could not raise a palm in farewell, but, like a man already ashamed, kneed his mount to take him more swiftly out of her sight over the fell.

It took till the dusk to get up to the peat moss, scarred with black trenches and fail-dikes of sods, the pattern made by that wee man Farrell's last honest work. Will Armstrong found himself sweating and squinting about as if the peewit trailing her wing were an omen, the shape of the clouds as the sky turned bloody, a warning. As they rode to the door, past the new mound of the grave, a crouched hare bolted from under the hooves of the Old Man's mount. 'Ho-Hoaah!' he sawed at the reins as it reared in alarm.

At that Will Armstrong cried, 'Let's go no further! Turn back from this road!'

The Old Man? He lashed his steed to a stand and sneered at his son. 'When the hare runs from me? Stop your shivering. We'll pass the night here, and at dawn we'll ride on to the river and cross at the ford.'

Did Will Armstrong think of his warm bed and young wife as he hunched on the step of that hovel and heard the rats run? He found that he did. Part of his wooing had been to boast of his deeds. Now he stared into the darkness, tormented with loathing to touch again her white breasts with hands bloody with this.

Anne Eliot, Anne Eliot . . . It sweetens my lips with the taste of wild heather honey to speak her fair name. Let me lick them slowly . . . Lust's a cruel barb, I should swallow the salt and spit in shame. But it's a window on the chalice of worship that lies in each man. Would ye not say so? That adoration . . . Aye, pass the salt-cellar. Here! I'll swallow a shovel of it! Mother of Love! Open the door! I'll retch in the yard . . .

Aye, tell the truth of it, it's lust sours the wine. Still, to speak of her . . . She watched from the gate as Will and the Old Man rode on that day. The wedding was done. Her wifely duty? The seal on the transaction of chattel and goods between the Old Man and her father, she knew well enough. To bear sons to be buried? Was it enough? For no woman. Lovely Anne Eliot . . . When the two riders pass out of sight, does she turn back to the household seeking the keys to each kist of pewter and linen to hang at her girdle? Call the wench in the kitchen to task? Pour scorn on each crither more lowly that came in her path? No. She stood in the linen of her wedding shift and strayed to the field's edge. There she wandered, plucking the cockle, the barley, the poppy and the white dog daisy. She crouched to watch the partridge run with her brood, their round bodies bobbing, and saw the mouse with its swivering tail clamber the stalks.

She drew these things to her and returned to the tower. And that night, her bed empty of Will, she sat in her chamber with what she had garnered. And there, plaited the stalks. Though she set some aside to bend into a corn rattle for her first child. Scattered flowers and barley lay on the bed until Anne's nimble fingers had woven a garland.

Ah, lovely child. She stands at her mirror crowned with the flowers. It was then that she saw a woman behind her, her eyes stern and tender, nodding her head. Did she turn, knowing the chamber was empty? No, she stood awhile longer with peace in her heart.

But where's peace for our lad? Bare, shivering, he squats in the circlet of light, the garland of flames, each knobbed bone of his spine fingered by cold and the breath of the stars. Can he get warm? His round knees, his chest, his belly and face take the tinge of red charcoal until he draws back. He turns, eyes the bed of sprung heather with its one dingy rug. Oh, he'd have been glad of it, right enough. But it's out in the shadow where he's warned not to step. So what has he left? The sword, a heel of the bread, and a swish in the flask . . .

Nothing comes. Nothing stirs. The night moves in slow quiet. He fidgets, plucks at small pebbles, tosses them to the fire as if to mock the whin's glow, like a child skimming stones on a river who makes no more than a tap on the water, shrugs his shoulders, watches it flow and gives the bit laugh.

Flying things buzz. He hears the high whine, how it seems to dance in his lugs. It would set him to scratching! But the smoke keeps them off.

Once, he stands, stretches, holds his pizzle, makes water, then rubs at his neck. When he sits, his chin nods to his chest. His lids close. And he sleeps.

What jerked him awake? The howl of a bairn, a bairn that howled with the cry that trembles the tongue. For all that he's naked, Martin jumped to his feet. His blood froze. There's a woman, aye, in the shadow nursing this hapless infant. Was it that set him shivering? No. Nor shame to stand with no clothes. It seemed that he knew her, knew how the silk of her long chestnut hair would feel in his grasp, knew the smell of her breath, her lips, her white neck. And the babe that she held? Hah! Who would not wish that howling to stop!

Martin Farrell, can he unclench his jaw? Hear how it clicked.

'Lady,' he stammered, 'come to the fire, warm yourself and your child.'

'Martin,' she said sweetly, 'will ye no come to me and give me a kiss?'

The lad? To have been in her arms, he knew would be bliss. The whin flared with a blue flame. He shook his head.

Then the wraith shook her head sadly. 'I cannot come to ye, though the babe I can pass. Will you comfort the bairn, hold him in your arms?'

Again our lad shook his head. 'Step into the light and I'll do what ye ask!'

With a sigh like the shiver of wind in an ash, she stepped forward and held out the bairn. Our lad lifted the infant against his bare chest. What did he find? The howling had stopped! He glanced down. Away! It seems that he's hugging his own naked ribs!

With a gasp, he looked up, but the woman was gone. 'Peace on ye, mother . . .' said Bess Graham's son.

Slowly, he kneeled and gazed into the fire, seeing each detail of her vanished face. Aye, and he mourned that it was all he had of her, but it was more of a treasure than the wee finger ring.

The stars slowly turn. There's dew on the grass. The white owl in the valley floats as silent as the grey moth. It seems our lad was alone, aye, and he's thinking if that was the shade the Crow warned me of, then I'm glad to have done as he said.

His mood lightened. With his elbows pressed on his knees, his chin cupped in his hand, he rested his head. But yet he's haunted by the deeds of his kin and the place of his word in this cruel feud. Longing for company, he ate the Crow's bread, had a wet from the flask. As he put back the stopper he heard a new sound out in the darkness, and there's a hot odour catches his breath. The stench of some beast. Still as the leveret, he strains to hear more. One hand creeps to the hilt of the sword, with the other he reaches for a brand from the fire. Half crouching, he stood and peered into the night, eyes blinking the flame dazzle. Crossing the moor, there slouched, half-walking, half-crawling, the brute fetch. The fetch the fiddler had tried to stake from his path, half boar and half man, the tusked peat-cutter came. He grunted, and swore, gave shrieks shrill with pain, and stumbled towards Martin, the curved daggers of teeth thrusting up from his jaw, bright with wet slobber.

Whisht! Did our lad know what he saw? No! In mortal terror he backed to the fire, his knuckles white as he raised the brand and the sword, and now the beast circled, again and again. Martin never once took his eyes from it, and strove to find courage to call the fetch in. Red-rimmed eyes. A black mane of bristles across shoulders and nape. It snouted the air, clocked and chopped with its teeth. Then Martin saw, draped on its back, a familiar scarf, the wee bit of rag Farrell had worn to cover his scars. The fetch clawed at the air with two sharp cloven hooves, but its feet? Martin stared. The broad calloused toes tanned yellow with peat!

Was it compassion that loosened Martin's tongue to call the beast in? No, I'd not say so. They circled again. Fear. Fear, that the night would never end. That he'd stay in this place forever and dawn would not come.

So he cried, 'Warm yourself at the fire! Mother o' Mercy! Do me no harm! Come into the light, and I'll do as ye want!'

The fetch? It staggered two steps and a third, and there, at our lad's feet it sank to its knees, grunting glabber, slashing its foul head from side to side. In the groan and the shriek of its speech, Martin heard words.

'Cut me in twa! Cut me in twa! For the day I bought ye a hat of ripe cherries cut me in twa!'

Invite them in and do as they ask . . .

Into a sky as black as the crow's tatters, Martin hefted the sword. Starlight ran on its edge as he kept his word. His body juddered from the crack of that blow and he staggered as the black boar charged free. Away! It's jinked by him and into the night. The man, Farrell? With a whisper of 'Peace on ye, I did little for ye,' faded from sight.

'And on ye,' Martin murmured. 'I'd forgotten the cherries you brought back from the fair in your hat . . .'

Hush . . . Look. There's a light. Does our lad see it? His head is bowed. He stares at the cleft in the ground by the fire he's made with the sword. A wraith tall and shimmering, nodded and watched.

'Hah! So you chose to seek your own path.'

Our lad? He gave the bit laugh. 'Fiddler! There's wine in the flask? I thought I'd left ye!'

'Aye,' says the fiddler. 'It seemed that ye did. So then, that was your route beyond the cross roads.'

Our lad? He saw the hurt palms, the deep bloody wounds. He ran towards him, wanting to help those grievous sores.

But the fiddler cried, 'Ware! Stay in the light!' When he saw Martin stagger and come to a halt, he nodded his head. 'Aye, I sleep on cold ground.'

'Then I ask ye, come to the fire and get warm.'

With that, the tall shade of the traveller crossed from the night and he stretched himself down with all that long grace he had. 'Ah, it's good . . .' He smiled at our lad.

Martin Farrell, with grief in his eyes, reached out to touch the blood on his palms, the gaping wound where the cloth was torn on his shirt.

'Away!' said the fiddler. 'I brought that on myself. I brought that on me on the day I saw my brother take to his horse. Would ye hear the tale? Sit, and be calm.'

Martin did what was asked. If it could be had, why, he'd have stayed in that companionable quiet for the rest of his life! Aye! Do you doubt it? Bare as Adam, he sat without shame, and in the darkest hour of the night, he listened, grew warm.

'I was born the second son of a high noble clan, in a fine

hall, and friends at both courts. I loved my father, my mother, our land, and our name. Yet I envied my brother, Martin, for each thing I won at, he'd won before me. Then it came to a day when one Yuletide there's arranged a great feast and the hunt of the stag.

'There's snow! Great fires in the hearth. All spits turning save the one that would stand ready for the meat they would bring. And my father says, no, you're too young. Stay with your mother.

'I went to the stableyard, saw the men mount. The steam of their breath, the glint of each spear, the flash of silk lining my brother's cloak of fur.'

The fiddler grew silent. The flame in the whin seemed to sink lower. 'As he swung up in his saddle, he'd eyes for nothing but the pride of my father. But I saw the girth of his saddle was frayed by the buckle. Another thread tore as he pushed his foot in the stirrup. As he reached for the reins that I held, yet another sprang from the leather. Martin Farrell, I held my tongue. They rode from the gate. At the height of the chase, that saddle girth broke, and my brother was thrown from the horse to his death . . . I left the same night. Took to the road. I played the fiddle until I once again learned the use of my tongue . . .'

Our lad from the moors, he sat long in thought. 'You must have loved him, to have taken the way that you chose . . .'

'Hah!' cried the fiddler, 'as each Cain loves his Abel before he lifts the rock!' He sat up, gazed at the sky, the fading night stars. Then he held out the fiddle with her curved neck, the bow, strung, greased and taut. 'Martin Farrell, my hands are too bloody. Will you play for me the song of regret?'

'Would ye ask it?' cried Martin. 'I canna! Don't ask me! I

can hack wi' this sword, and that's newly learned. I can build a fire, make a snare, sort and stack the dry sod and the wet. Find a nest, tell ye where the rain comes from when there's a wind . . .'

'Then I must leave ye.'

'No! I left ye before.' Martin reached for the fiddle, and the Galloway man smiled the bit smile, walked to stand behind him, and in that embrace helped him tuck the wood to his chin and hold, light in his fingers, the horse-hair bow.

For the sake of his friend, Martin tried the first note. Aye, there's a sound, wild, high and lonely. The cry of the geese in the skein stitching autumn to spring each year round. And it stayed all the while Martin drew the bow down. A light touch from the fiddler's fingers oiled his wrists. Some grace was set in them. Then Martin played all he had loved and would leave with regret. The wind bowing the grass, the wren's sudden bright trill, the wet flank of the calf, slimed and licked into life. The paw by paw stalking of the wildcat bitch as she hunts the white hare through the snow. The accurate flurry and speckle of blood as she pounces.

He played the black crayfish that shoots back under stones, the hunger that hunts it till finger ends shrivel and numb. The bee at the heather, its chanter pipe drone, the ringing of curlews, the stone-chat tapping like stones.

Ah, Martin Farrell. What he played for the fiddler was mostly his own. When did the wraith leave him? As he played the huge sky? Entranced by the fiddle, Martin played on. The dark of midwinter, when the sun's a red eye, the scudding clouds boil and the mists of the Spring. The low wind of midsummer, the salt Solway breeze that spices the heather. And the moon high all day long above Autumn's leaves.

He played the grey light, lit by one star, the set of the moon and the first pale line between night and the moor. The whin crumpled to ash, stalk by stalk, flower by gold flower, as the rising sun trembled and mist rose from the river.

Then his fiddle fell silent as the dawn took his song. Our lad? He stared in wonder, for he found he stood on a green mossy knoll, by the grey bed of a fire ringed by grey stones, where red sparks still showed in the feather-soft ash. And there was the river, aye, no dry bed of a stream, but the river, down from the ford, where a deeply cut pool shaded by thickets of trees and of fern, sheltered the brown speckled trout.

Had he dreamed? I'd not say so. He looked at the fiddle, the bow. Where the Crow's bed had been there was a bent thorn tree with a long black tatter of cloth caught in its arms. Martin walked from the circle and tugged the length down. Until he had better he'd take that for his clothes. Naked? Tired? Aye, he was, but his spirit was high.

Again, he set the wood to his chin, and played a few notes. Were they as wild and sweet as they'd rung in the night? I'd say they gave the wee falter, but still were in tune. And that's Martin's delight. That is, till he turns and sees the sword on the ground. He swore softly. For all his night's work, it seemed no fetch had broken that bond.

With a sigh he took all he owned to the edge of the pool, left cloth, fiddle, bow and sword on the bank, and plunged into the water. He swam and he drank, and rubbed his hair clean.

Who else heard those notes? The Old Man and Will riding down to the ford. And Hughie Graham. It made the stoat shiver where he rode up the Rigg. He tethered his mount and crept low through the gorse.

Still Martin swam as the rising sun drew the mist from the water leaving it clear as a mirror. The spray glittered from him as he came to the surface and broke through its glass.

High above him, towering on horseback, Old Man Armstrong laughed. 'Look, Will, it seems we must fish . . .' Clad in his jack-coat of leather and mail, he swung down from his horse, bent one knee to kneel among the bushes and studied our lad.

Martin stared from him to Will, but Will Armstrong winced and fixed his own gaze between the ears of his horse.

'Do you know who I am?'

The cinder grey beard. The cold cruel squint. Aye, to be sure, Martin Farrell did.

Yet the lad stood in the water, silent as death, shaking his head. And what was he thinking? His thoughts whirled like the water that swirled from the pool, like the leaves that rode with the current to crash down the fall. He searched through the deeds of the night for what might come to his aid. Glancing about, 'Neb Corbie!' he cried.

'Hah! Ye think me Wull O' The Shroud?' The Old Man held out his mailed hand for Martin to grasp. 'Come here, and I'll teach you my name.'

Martin turned and swam from him back to the bank where the sword lay. His flanks juddered with cold, water dripped from his fingers as he grasped the hilt. It seemed fate had crossed him and like a fly he'd been caught in its dark woven web. So he waited, as the two men on horseback splashed through the ford.

And what of Hughie, crouched in the gorse. He was cursing, to see all the prey he might want and not have his wolves with him. Aye, and trembling for fear of being seen.

At a slow trot, the Armstrongs bore down, then Will

kicked his horse on and caught at the reins of the Old Man. 'You'll no slay him naked?'

'Then lend him your shirt.'

Will hissed, 'Look, how he stands. He's no beard. See him! He waits like a man!'

'That's Armstrong blood in him . . . He's been with the Widow. I know that sword.' And with that, Old Man Armstrong climbed down from his horse.

With the whisper of iron, he drew his own blade.

'Father,' said Martin.

'You've got none, egg of a viper. What she hatched I won't rear!'

Our lad, he chanced at Will Armstrong. 'Brother?' he cried. And, aye, give him his due, Will's fingers burned to the knuckle to reach for his sword. 'Nails o' God! I'm of the same seed!'

This man, this Armstrong, swung at the lad. The blade hummed. Each thing has its tune.

That's when the boar charged. Black, bristling, it burst from the whins and with a slash and a chop sliced Armstrong's leg. He toppled, crashed to the ground, with the heart's blood a fountain that leapt from his thigh. Again the brute slashed, stamping and hot, at his throat and his ear. Will leapt from his horse to drive the beast off and Martin ran with his sword, but the demon's away!

Now the tune's changed. The night held the key. Slashed and bleeding to death, the Old Man lies on the earth. The harvest sun stares in his eyes, as they dim. Had he last words? If he had no one heard as Will tore at the cloth of his shirt to twist on the wounds. 'What are ye?' he cried, 'that ye can call on such aid?'

Let's not forget Hughie Graham. He smiled, gave over

cursing and starts blessing the day. He crept closer, watching the bare nape of Will's neck, where he was bent, tugging off his belt for a binding to keep the heart's blood from pulsing out of these wounds.

Our lad? Whisht. He watches in pity the blood dabble Will's shirt. 'I needed no aid,' he said, calmly. The shock of the truth gave him his words. 'I was no more than a tool, forged in the womb, to put an end to this feud. I've no gift for sight, but I see he wrote his own fate, in deed after deed.'

Will Armstrong stood and gazed at the lad. 'What's your name?'

'I've got none.' Martin held out the sword. 'Will you take it?'

There's a flash on the blade. ''Ware. What's this?' Will Armstrong, grabbed the hilt, turned and pushed Martin aside! What had he seen? The glint of Hughie Graham's weapon as he'd crept up behind. Oh! I could wax merry on the death of the stoat! The poisoner, the sneaker, the creeper, the plotter, the flatterer, there's no blood in his veins but the poison of greed. He's no match for Will Armstrong's broad arms and great burning beard! The fool ran to his fate felled by the edge of a sharp Graham blade with a scream like a hare.

Away! The tale's done. Snuff out the tallows. Open the door. Let in the cold air. Listen? Can ye hear it? The *drap, drap* of the thaw? The commotion of rooks at their squabble of nests? Hoo! Breathe deep of that! The sweet damp loam . . . Let the bairns run to seek out the purple bud of the crocus when the sun's up.

Whisht! Would you have me tie every knot? A man on a grey mare rode over the knoll, he gave me – will ye pass it? – my hat. Breeks and boots I've worn out on the road.

Wull O' The Shroud? He trod the corpse road with Will Armstrong as he took home his load. And the first time I played my fiddle in a hall was at the great feast Will Armstrong gave for Anne Eliot at the birth of their child.

So then. Would ye have one last tune? Pass me the fiddle, aye, and I'll play ye one of my own.